Gathering Home

A Deep South Book

Reprinted paperback edition published by
The University of Alabama Press, 1999
The University of Alabama Press
Tuscaloosa, Alabama 35487-0380
Manufactured in the United States of America

Cover design by Shari DeGraw

∞

The paper on which this book is printed meets the minimum
requirements of American National Standard for Information
Science-Permanence of Paper for Printed Library Materials,
ANSI Z39.48-1984.

Library of Congress Cataloging-in-Publication Data

Covington, Vicki.
Gathering Home / Vicki Covington.
p.   cm.
"A Deep South book"—P. preceding t.p.
ISBN 0-8173-1002-9 (alk. paper)
1. Teenagers—Alabama—Fiction.
2. Adoptees—Alabama—Fiction. I. Title
PS3553.O883G37   1999
813´.54—dc21   99-20122

British Library Cataloguing-in-Publication data available

For Dennis

ACKNOWLEDGMENTS

The author wishes to express gratitude to her husband, Dennis Covington; her parents, Jack and Katherine Marsh; Daniel Menaker, Nancy Nicholas, Amanda Urban, Randy and Haden Marsh, Robert and Mary Frances Bailey, Howard Cruse and Ed Sedarbaum, and the Alabama State Council on the Arts—for their help and support.

O N E

Whitney was beside the pool. The woman in the chaise longue next to her had been chain-smoking, using a fancy holder. First, she asked Whitney if she was interested in religion. "Of course," Whitney answered. What choice was there, being the daughter of a clergyman? They moved on to the question of heaven and hell, to speaking in tongues, and now to angels.

"Do you believe in them?" the woman asked.

"Yeah, I guess so."

"Have you ever seen one?"

"No," Whitney said.

"Well, I have. And let me tell you, they are *big.*"

Whitney began peeling her nail polish. It fell to the poolside in tiny coral flakes. After a polite period of time had passed—enough so that her departure would not appear rude and abrupt—Whitney gathered her towel and suntan oil and said goodbye. Once, when she was young, Whitney had seen God. It was a man's face in the sky. She ran inside to tell her mother, who was frying okra. "Good," her mother said with nonchalance. It might as well have been the postman. Of course, Whitney later reasoned that it was only a formation of clouds that created the image. And nothing else strange had ever happened to her. In fact, Whitney was bored. These conferences, especially, bored her. This year, the conference was in New Orleans. Whitney hoped it would be more fun because of the trouble between the moderates and fundamentalists. Whitney's parents were moderates. They pastored a progressive, urban church in Birmingham. Whitney was obligated to attend some sessions, since she was one of the representatives from her church and was expected to be informed on the pressing issues.

"Who cares about school prayer, abortion, and evolution," Whitney's mother said, "when the world is starving and our Hispanic neighbors are being murdered?"

"Sanctuary," her father said quietly.

Whitney was tired of the word. And maybe a bit annoyed by the Gautemalan girl who had shared her bedroom last winter.

In the hotel room, this conversation was interrupted by a phone call. Cal, Whitney's father, stood by the window that overlooked Canal Street. He was wearing khaki pants and a crinkled one-hundred-percent cotton shirt. Whitney wished her parents would get away from earth colors. They always looked dressed for a safari.

"Right," Cal said into the telephone. "Yes, right. Right." Pause. "Right." He said "right" a lot. He was a nice guy. He had a baritone voice. Cal winked at Whitney and said, "Right, O.K., right," into the phone.

Whitney took a sideways glance at herself when she passed the mirror. Her swimsuit was black with big geometric designs—great colors like chartreuse and purple. She liked her body a lot. In fact, she couldn't take her eyes off herself.

In the bathroom, her mother, Mary Ellen, was all wrapped up in a towel, blow-drying her hair. The room was steamy. Mary Ellen had the heat lamp on. Hotels were great, Whitney thought. This one was anyway. Whitney had seen some bad ones. Mary Ellen grabbed a tube of Whitney's lipstick and dabbed it on lightly. It was almost a grape color. It looked good on Mary Ellen. Mary Ellen used Whitney's makeup sometimes but never bought it for herself. She didn't need it. People had always told Whitney that her mother looked like Natalie Wood. Whitney knew that Natalie Wood was a movie star whose films were made a while back—mostly before Whitney was born. Whitney believed that Natalie Wood was dead now, but she wasn't sure. She'd never heard anybody compare her father to a movie star but she did know, for a fact, that women fell in love with him. She could tell when one of the church women was falling. She'd say something stupid to Whitney like, "Your father is a dear, dear person," with Cal standing right there. Why couldn't they just tell him instead of talking through her? And the worst part was when they looked at *her* with sparkly eyes like *she* was the one they were falling in love with. It was awful.

"I met a weird lady at the pool," Whitney said.

"Weird in what way?" Mary Ellen asked.

"She's seeing angels."

Mary Ellen tilted her head to one side, then to the other, then back again, as if to say, "Well, maybe she is seeing them."

"Mom, she's really crazy. She weighed about ninety

pounds and was smoking cigarettes in this little thing—
what are they called? And she said the angels were real
big. Her eyes were spooky, too."

"Is she part of the conference?"

"Probably. There are a lot of strange people here,
you know."

"What do you find particularly strange?"

Whitney shrugged. She was tired of talking to Mary
Ellen's reflection in the mirror; not tired of Mary Ellen,
just the steamy place, the situation. "I'm going to take a
shower," she said. She stepped out of her swimsuit and
tried hard to avoid gazing at her bare, wonderful self in
the mirror. In the shower, she washed her hair with
lemon-scented shampoo. Using Cal's razor, she shaved
her legs, then marveled at her tan—the color contrast
where her swimsuit line came. Her legs were like but-
terscotch, her hips vanilla ice cream. Whitney stood
under the water a long time.

Afterward, she put on a boring dress—white with
oval buttons. "Sweet" is what some people might have
said about this dress. But Whitney was going to dinner
with her parents. And, being Cal's daughter, she had
learned to play the part. If there was one thing she
could do well, it was play the part. It was something
she'd learned from Cal and Mary Ellen. Whitney knew
from the real acting she'd done over the years—she
was on fire for drama—that the ties you developed
being in a play with someone were deep and strong. So,
in this way, she believed her family was very close.

The restaurant was on a mezzanine that overlooked
the hotel lobby. It had a big open atrium with fountains
and gardens. In the center was a bar. Whitney sat by
the railed edge so she could peer down at the people.
Directly below her, a man was playing a baby grand.

Whitney looked at the menu. Crawfish étouffée.
Blackened redfish. Jambalaya. Shrimp creole. When

the waitress came, Whitney ordered a hamburger.

"Toppings?" the waitress asked.

"What?"

"Toppings. You have a choice of sliced jalapeño peppers, salsa, chili, tasso ham, olives, mushrooms, sautéed onions. Your cheeses are cheddar, Swiss, American, mozzarella, and boursin."

"I'll just have some mustard and ketchup, please."

"No cheese?"

"No, thank you."

Mary Ellen and Cal ordered jambalaya.

"I couldn't understand her," Whitney told them. "She's got a funny accent."

"She's Cajun," Cal said.

"Isn't she lovely?" Mary Ellen said.

They always said something nice about people from other countries or cultures. It was real predictable. They ran conversational English classes at their church back in Birmingham. They knew a lot of languages. When Cal and Mary Ellen were first married, they wanted to be missionaries in China. Whitney was grateful this didn't happen. She hated to imagine what it would have been like to have grown up in China. She would have stood out like a sore thumb with her blond hair. Mary Ellen knew American Sign Language, too. They had many deaf members in the congregation. Every Sunday, Mary Ellen signed Cal's sermons to the deaf people. Whitney watched her mother the entire hour. It was fascinating. Mary Ellen wore a hat on Sunday. She had all kinds of hats. She was fashion-conscious when it came to hats, Whitney thought.

Cal took Whitney's hand. "Having fun?"

Whitney smiled and looked away. They all knew the answer.

"Well, we appreciate your being so kind to everyone, especially last night," Cal said. Last night was the opening session of the conference. There was a big reception—ministers, their wives, and children. A ballroom of actors. Whitney occasionally caught the eye of other girls her age. They knew the secret, too—smile and act like nothing's wrong. "There are a lot of people looking to us for strength," Mary Ellen had told her in what Whitney considered to be one of her mother's weaker moments. Generally, Mary Ellen avoided this kind of talk. Nevertheless, it was true. Their phone rang at crazy hours. Cal left home frequently during the night. Mary Ellen's prayer list often had over two hundred names. Cal and Mary Ellen dealt with this issue in one of their books, *The Twenty-Five Hour Day: Stress in the Parsonage.* On the jacket of the book was a picture of Cal and Mary Ellen. It said something about how they were born in Alabama and met in seminary, married in 1967, have one daughter—Whitney—and have co-authored several books. The most recent one, which was to be published in the fall, was called *Sanctuary.* It was dedicated to the Guatemalan girl who had lived in Whitney's bedroom last winter.

The waitress brought the iced tea. It was served with mint leaves instead of lemon. "Listen," Cal said as he added sugar to his tea. "Why don't you take tomorrow for yourself? Go to the Quarter, take the streetcar to the zoo, something fun."

It sounded great.

"There's no need for you to be here for tomorrow's session. Essentially, it will be a big fight. I don't want to put you through it."

"Good," Whitney said.

"You can shop," Mary Ellen added.

"I do want you to understand what's going on in the Conference, though," Cal continued. "You understand that a certain faction is trying to take over the Conference, trying to tell everyone what to believe, how to vote, trying to muddy the division of church and state."

"Mom!" Whitney said to Mary Ellen. "There she is. There's the woman who saw an angel." The woman was alone, leaning over a rail, staring at the lobby below. She was wearing a gold dress, smoking the longest cigarette Whitney had ever seen.

Whitney had studied the map she got from the hotel concierge's desk. Whitney liked maps. She liked to know where she was going. Leaving the hotel, she stepped out onto Canal Street. The early-morning traffic was heavy. Buses stormed the median that was lined with crepe myrtle. She crossed Canal, and things got narrow. She was in the French Quarter. It reminded her of being in a dollhouse, only it was too dirty for that. Men with giant garbage bins were busy with trash. Others were hosing the sidewalks. There was a bad smell. She was standing at the curb where Royal and Bienville intersect when she saw a dead baby pigeon. She shuddered and took Bienville over to Chartres. Up ahead was the steeple of the cathedral. The sight of it helped. Plus this was the landmark her father had told her to find. It meant she was close to Jackson Square, her first destination of the morning.

Whitney liked it at once. The Square was all green grass with marigolds and petunias. It was enclosed by a black wrought-iron fence. Sidewalks ran the perimeter, lined with shops that had big long windows, allowing Whitney a great view of herself. She had on new jams. Glancing at each window, she tried to look at things inside—porcelain carousels, brass animals, carnival masks. She sat on a bench and drew her legs up so her chin rested on her knees. Her kneecaps were fuzzy like fresh peaches. She sat a long time, looking at the artists setting up easels. She was particularly interested in the portraits.

She crossed over to Cafe du Monde and got some beignets and orange juice. Coal barges moved at a snail's pace along the river. Horse-drawn carriages lined the street, but nothing was going on yet in the Quarter. It was too early. She decided to go back to the hotel. She took Royal to Canal. At the hotel entrance, a bellhop opened the door. The lobby was fresh and cool. Water cascaded over rock tiers in the fountain. The friendly concierge who gave her the map said hello to her. Piano music was all over the atrium.

Whitney took the elevator to the second floor—the one designated for meetings. All the conference rooms were named for bodies of water. There was the Mediterranean, the Baltic, Aegean, Caribbean. Each one was packed with people. It took her a moment to figure it out—they were all watching TV monitors of the conference, which was taking place in the big, overflowing ballroom. She walked into the grand room. People were packed in like sardines. It looked like political conventions she'd seen on TV, only without the balloons and confetti. She spotted the Alabama delegation and Mary Ellen's big scarlet hat. People appeared distracted and a bit agitated. Whitney sensed there was something afoot, so she decided to check things out. Always an outside chance somebody might do something out of the ordinary. She got three sweetrolls from the tray beside the coffee urn and walked toward her mother's red hat. She said, "Excuse me, please," and smiled her Sunday smile as she made her way to Mary Ellen. There were no empty seats, so she sat cross-legged on the floor in front of Mary Ellen's chair. People were milling about, and no one was at the podium.

"What's going on?" Whitney said to Mary Ellen.

"This is a coffee break. I thought you were out walking. Anything wrong?"

"I just decided to stop by the meeting," Whitney said.

Mary Ellen stroked Whitney's hair. "That's nice of you," she said. For a second, she eyed Whitney's turquoise jams.

"I'm sorry," Whitney whispered. "Should I go to the room and change?"

"Not unless you want to," Mary Ellen said. "Everybody's too involved to notice."

"Where's Dad?"

"He's going to speak in a while."

Mary Ellen handed Whitney a conference program. She examined it carefully, searching for Cal's name to see if her name was there, too. She liked it when the biographical information said: He has one daughter, Whitney. But there were no names or blurbs on this one. She gave it back to Mary Ellen.

"I went for a walk," Whitney said.

"Where to?"

"The Square. I had some beignets."

"And now three sweetrolls," Mary Ellen added.

Whitney grinned and looked away.

"Did you find any clothes shops?" Mary Ellen asked.

"I think the clothes here are weird. They all look like costumes. Did you and Dad ever come to Mardi Gras?"

"No."

Whitney looked at her legs. "Is my tan fading?"

Mary Ellen patted Whitney's head. "You look like a little gingerbread man. You're fine."

Whitney looked at Mary Ellen's scarlet hat and bright eyes. Her mother wasn't like anybody else's mother.

"Is Dad speaking soon?" Whitney asked, examining her legs again. There was a nick on her shin from Cal's razor.

"He may be next. It all depends. See those men over there?" Mary Ellen pointed to a table near the podium. "They're in charge. Whatever they say is what goes." They all looked alike to Whitney—wearing burgundy blazers. They looked like Shriners.

"I think I'll go upstairs for a while," Whitney said.

"O.K., honey."

Whitney took the elevator to the fifteenth floor. She walked down the hallway until she reached 1508, their room. She opened the door. Maid service had obviously been in. The beds were made. She turned on the TV.

An old Western was on. She changed channels but couldn't find anything other than news, weather, and cartoons.

There was a stack of papers by the lamp on the nightstand. They were covered with Cal's handwriting —tiny hieroglyphic markings. Whitney wondered why he wrote like that. It was so hard to read. She could make out a heading that said "A Table for the Hungry," with various scriptures beside it. Notes for the sermon he'd deliver back in Birmingham next Sunday. In her mind, Whitney saw Mary Ellen's hands signing "table" then "hungry" for the deaf people.

Whitney opened the nightstand drawer. There was a New Orleans telephone directory and underneath it a stack of hotel stationery. Whitney saw that Mary Ellen had begun a letter. "Dear Maria," it said. She tried hard to avoid reading it, but her eyes carried her into the letter. "We are in New Orleans. We are all fine. Whitney is out of school for the summer. I'm sure she misses you, just as Cal and I do. We pray for your safety and happiness. After all the anguish you've endured, surely there will be solace."

The letter ended there, unfinished. Whitney put the telephone directory back over the stationery and closed the drawer. She wasn't quite sure what her mother meant by "the anguish" Maria had "endured." All Whitney could recall was her broken English, dark eyes, and the way she spooned tiny servings of food onto her plate at dinner. Whitney tried to get her interested in ice cream, chocolates, and pastries—but Maria didn't have a sweet tooth or something. In the afternoons after school, Whitney was involved with the theater—all winter. And in the evenings, Maria went to bed early. Whitney didn't spend much time with her. In fact, she hardly knew her at all, if you got right down to it.

Whitney pulled a chair up to the window and stared at the pool terrace below. There were several glasstop tables underneath big umbrellas, and huge planters filled with greenery. A boy was feverishly swimming laps in the pool as if he were in a race—only there was no competition. Whitney heard the key click into the lock and saw, in the mirror, Cal and Mary Ellen coming in. They seemed to be moving slowly as if they were tired or maybe even a bit sick.

"Hi," Whitney said, turning toward them.

Mary Ellen tossed her scarlet hat onto the bed and smiled half-heartedly at Whitney. She came over to where Whitney was standing and looked down at the terrace. Her eyes were distant and misty. Whitney knew this look. It was disturbing—partly because Whitney didn't understand it. Certain topics brought it on, like sanctuary and the hearing-impaired, and bumper stickers that said things like "Arts Balance Children." Sometimes she had the look during a cantata. But then it might appear at the sight of a table that needed dusting or a crooked lampshade.

"The meeting didn't go as we'd hoped," Mary Ellen said. Whitney looked at the pool. From the side of the terrace directly under their window, the angel woman appeared. She sat down in a chaise longue.

"There she is again, Mom," Whitney said, pointing to the woman.

"Who?"

"The woman who sees angels."

"We could use some angels at this conference."

Whitney knew she should ask questions about the meeting, but she didn't know what to ask. It was the same with Maria. It was like if you don't know where to start, you just think of something else instead.

Whitney looked at her mother. She decided to give it a try. "What happened at the meeting?" she asked.

Cal came over to her. He put a hand on her shoulder. "Look down there," he said, motioning toward the terrace. "Now, we're both looking in the same direction, right? But we may see different things. Like, you may see your angel woman," he said and smiled at her. "And I might see that taxi over on Canal Street behind the terrace. Understand what I'm getting at?"

"Not really."

"Remember the men in charge?" Mary Ellen asked her. "The ones at the podium?"

The Shriners. "Yeah, I remember."

"They want us all to interpret the Bible the same way. They want us all to think alike," Mary Ellen said.

"That's impossible," Whitney said.

"Yes, it is," Cal agreed. "There are other things, too. Like they don't think that women should be ordained to preach. And they want to stop children from reading certain books."

"What books?"

"There's a long list."

Cal took her hand. "This is a difficult time," he said. Then he walked to the closet, took off his safari shirt, and hung it up. Mary Ellen sat on the edge of the bed and took off her red pumps. Whitney looked at the floor. They were like a cast, Whitney felt, offstage between acts. They were all out of character temporarily, and it was suddenly disconcerting—the sight of her father's bare chest and her mother's feet, nobody knowing what to say.

"I want some raw oysters," Whitney said.

Cal turned and, predictably, smiled. "You don't like raw oysters," he said.

"I want to learn to eat them."

"They ooze down your throat like big egg yolks," Mary Ellen warned. It was like a dare. Whitney couldn't stand eggs in any form. Then more seriously Mary Ellen said, "Why do you want to learn to eat them?"

"You know. It's like developing a taste for coffee. It's just something I have to do eventually."

Cal looked at his watch. "It's a little early for lunch, don't you think?"

"I could eat now," Mary Ellen said.

"Who has good oysters?" Cal asked her.

"Felix's, maybe?"

Cal got his shirt off the hanger and put it back on. Whitney went to the bathroom and changed into a boring ivory dress. When she went back to the bedroom, Mary Ellen and Cal were all ready to go, dressed for the safari. They walked down the carpeted hallway, and Whitney pushed the elevator button. They stood and waited. Whitney began to dread the oysters, but she knew that Cal and Mary Ellen wouldn't make her eat more than she could stand the first time. In the elevator, she did what her parents were doing—she backed up against the rail so that there would be plenty of room for other people.

T W O

Whitney's parents adopted her near Ft. McClellan when Cal was stationed there as a chaplain. Her biological parentage didn't matter to her or anyone else until Cal decided to run for public office. Then, historical family details of any nature were suddenly surfacing as rapidly as the groundswell of Cal's candidacy. In Whitney's mind, though, they'd always been on some campaign trail—her father, her mother, and herself—being a family of the clergy. The only thing different now was a change in her mother's wardrobe from earth tones to rainbow colors, and her father began parting his hair on the left rather than the right.

She wasn't sure why he was running. The idea must have planted itself in his mind sometime during the conference in New Orleans two years ago because she recalled the conversation her parents had had that day at Felix's when she learned to eat oysters. Mary Ellen had told Cal that at least twenty people had cornered her after Cal spoke at the meeting—raving over his oratorical brilliance and asking questions about his politics.

"I told them you were not a political person," she'd told Cal.

Whitney watched as Mary Ellen mixed her own cocktail sauce, using the tiny paper cups the waitress had provided, apparently for this purpose. Mary Ellen used ketchup, Worcestershire, horseradish, and lemon juice. Whitney noted that the people at other tables also mixed their own concoctions. Cal just squeezed lemon juice on to his oysters and didn't fool with the sauce-mixing.

"I'm afraid," Cal said, "we're all being forced into politics whether we like it or not. It's the nature of the controversy within the Conference."

Whitney decided to just pour some straight ketchup onto her oysters. Mary Ellen smiled when she did it.

"Is this O.K.?" Whitney asked her.

"You do whatever makes it more palatable," Mary Ellen said and patted Whitney's hand. "Put the oysters on a cracker. That helps, too."

"Someone asked me if you've ever considered running for Congress," Mary Ellen said to Cal.

Cal smiled and swallowed an oyster with incredible ease. Whitney had marveled at this. "That would certainly go against our beliefs, wouldn't it?" he asked her.

"Which ones?" Mary Ellen asked.

"The basic one."

Mary Ellen nodded.

"What's that?" Whitney asked him.

"Separation of church and state, sweetie," Mary Ellen reminded her.

But the idea didn't die there at Felix's. Whitney heard rumblings all during the next year about the congressional representative elected from District 6 that fall. Apparently, he was one of the "Shriners," though Whitney never saw him, never knew if he wore a burgundy blazer. She just knew that Cal and Mary Ellen and members of their church wore pained expressions and talked about Moral Majority and how it had taken over not only the church conference but also the city. She overheard conversations Cal began having with men and women she'd never met, though she recognized one from the City Council and another from the TV local news. And one night, the mayor—he was black and just recently elected—came over, real late. She heard these people telling Cal he needed to run, that only a minister could pull it off—only a minister could knock off this new Bad-News Congressman, who was also a minister but was from the other camp. Whitney was busy with school and drama, and it took her by surprise when Cal appeared suddenly on the front page of the paper and on TV, saying he was a candidate—though he had, one morning, in the car, taking her to school, asked her what she would think about his running for Congress. She had shrugged, said, "Whatever," or something like that. It was just one more thing to get used to. Life with Cal was that way. A minister's home was a place where you rolled with the punches. You did distasteful things, made distasteful adjustments, and accustomed yourself to foreign ideas and people—like having a Guatemalan girl move into your bedroom or knowing that you might be moving to Washington next fall.

• • •

Their screened porch was built up high on a foundation of fieldstone, which gave Whitney a bird's-eye view of her neighborhood. Most of the children were young. Since she was beginning to understand things now, she realized that most parents with kids her age had moved to the suburbs to escape the city and the public school system. She reasoned that Cal and Mary Ellen might have moved, too, had she not gone to EPIC elementary school. EPIC stood for Educational Program for the Individual Child and was a good public school designed for special children. She was in a gifted class. Her schoolmates were alphabet-soup kids: LD, EMR, TMR, EC, deaf, in wheelchairs.

And then, after elementary school, she'd been accepted at the Fine Arts School—also part of the city system. On this morning in late November—with the trees having shed most of their leaves—she could actually see the taller downtown buildings from her screened porch atop Red Mountain that overlooked the city.

Cal was reading the newspaper in the white rocker next to hers. They wore lightweight jackets, but it was still warm enough to have breakfast on the porch—a Saturday morning family tradition. Whitney drew her legs up, propping her chin on her camel-colored corduroys. On the sidewalk, two girls rode by on bicycles. They looked ten, maybe. Across the street, the Hardys' youngest son was crawling in and out of a cardboard box. His yard was flecked with red and gold leaves.

Mary Ellen came out wearing a terry cloth bathrobe that Maria had sent her from Guatemala. It was black with orange and chartreuse designs. She put a tray of sausage and biscuits on the ledge, along with a pitcher of orange juice. She sat in the rocker. They were like The Three Bears, Whitney used to imagine, here in their respective rockers on Saturday mornings.

"A reporter asked me the other day if I believed that

young people today were, as a group, depressed," Cal said. "What do you think of that?"

"I think it's a stupid question," Whitney replied.

Cal smiled over at her. He looked like some singer she couldn't name—with his hair parted on the left now.

"What's stupid about it?" he asked her.

Whitney shrugged.

"Are *you* depressed?" Mary Ellen asked her. "Unhappy?"

Whitney looked up from her biscuit.

"Are you mad at him for running?" Mary Ellen asked, nodding toward Cal. Her mother was always getting to the heart of the matter.

Whitney grinned.

"What's the smile for?"

"It's just you. You're funny," Whitney said to her mother.

Cal looked pained. "I'm sorry," he said to Whitney.

"For what?"

"I should have talked more with you before I announced."

"Don't worry about it," she said.

Whitney spread some margarine and blackberry jam on her biscuit and poured up a glass of orange juice. Cal was always apologizing for something these days.

"It's all a year away," Whitney said. "I'll get used to the idea. I'm flexible. Being flexible is something you get used to, living in this house, you know," she said.

Cal reached over, resting his hand on the knee of her camel-colored corduroys. "I want you to know that I don't expect anything from you. You can stay as uninvolved as you like."

She knew his intentions were good.

"I will say one thing," Mary Ellen said. "You might want to stop by headquarters, though, after school one day. Just once, to see what it's like. Being in drama, you might find it interesting."

Light from the morning sun fell on Mary Ellen's face. Whitney knew that her mother was, in general, worth listening to.

Headquarters was a half-mile from her high school. She rode her bicycle past the old restored houses and new townhomes until she came to Five Points, where the streets and avenues met in a star. Her father's church sat in the heart of it. The architectural design was Spanish and quaint. But, in the shops nearby, they were placing purple neons in the windows and attaching new-wave awnings above the entrances. Whitney believed this to be a confused neighborhood. She could hear Cal's response to this accusation: "We are meeting the needs of the old and the young." Cal's headquarters was located in an office suite painted pale pink. It housed an attorney and a dentist, who were supporters of the campaign. Whitney went in. The walls were plastered with "Calvin Gaines for Congress" posters and bumper stickers—all red, white, and blue. There was a big map of District 6, an American flag, and a chalkboard with names of various neighborhoods in the city.

"Could I help you?" a man asked. He was at a desk, dialing on the telephone. He was all sooty like maybe he was a mechanic or something. Before Whitney could answer, a woman's voice called from behind her.

"Whitney!"

She turned.

It was Francy, her father's secretary from the church.

"This is Cal's daughter," she said to the mechanic. He stepped from behind the desk. He wore jeans. He had brown eyes, the kind that sparkle. Whitney decided he was cute, but too old for her.

"This is Nat," Francy said. "He's a steelworker. He's doing great things for the campaign."

Whitney gave Nat her best smile.

"So what can we put you to work doing?" Nat asked

and turned back to the desk where he began shuffling computer printout sheets. "Your eyesight good?"

Whitney opened her eyes wide. "Yes."

Nat led her to a long table and pulled out a chair. "Have a seat. These are names of registered voters in District 6," he said, handing her a printout. "This is a phone book," he said, smiled, and gave her a city directory. "We need phone numbers for all these people. See, the addresses are listed with the names on the printout, so you can match it up in the directory to make sure it's the right name and number. Understand?" Nat was up in her face now. She was ready to do anything he asked. He had a great scar over his right eyebrow.

Whitney worked for a solid hour. She liked doing it. It was methodical, and she considered herself a methodical person. She was doing the B's—Bailey, Baker, Banner, Baxley, Baylor. She wondered who had done the A's. She went to the other side of the partition where Francy was typing. "Who did the A's?" she asked. Francy looked up over her half-rimmed glasses. She was chewing gum feverishly.

"What, hon?"

"I'm doing the B's on the voter list. I was just curious about who did the A's."

Francy took the gum from her mouth, wrapped it in cellophane, and threw it into the trash can. She smiled at Whitney.

"The Union," she said.

"What union?"

"Steelworkers," Francy said, her tiny chocolate chip eyes darting like crazy. She stood up and took Whitney's shoulders. "Nat's got all the Union committed to the campaign. It's won-der-ful," Francy drawled.

Francy sat down at her typewriter and took all the rings off her skinny fingers. She began exercising each finger individually and energetically. Once, when Francy was typing a sermon for Cal called "Spiritual

Anorexia," she started crying and couldn't stop. That was what Cal had said, anyway.

Whitney went back to her table and began looking up numbers again. At four-thirty, a group of men came in, toting telephone directories. Whitney knew they were steelworkers. They had on caps that said Local 431. They sat at the end of Whitney's table and drank coffee from a thermos. They lit up cigarettes. Nat came over and introduced her as "Whitney." She was glad he didn't point out that she was the candidate's daughter.

Around five, things started happening. People filed into headquarters, and Francy popped up like a jack-in-the-box. Nat sat down beside Whitney and put his arm on the back of her chair.

"See that man?" he asked and pointed to a bald, rotund fellow. "He's an archeologist. Teaches at the University. The girl with him is a work-study student from Nigeria. They'll be great workers, you can tell."

Whitney watched Francy give the archeologist a kiss.

"Francy likes to kiss," Whitney said to Nat.

Nat looked at Whitney's mouth. "Francy's a case," he said. "That guy over there works at the zoo. He's an artist, too. He'll be designing all the posters. Looks like a renegade, doesn't he?"

Nat got up and met a group of women coming in the door. One woman handed him some printout sheets. Nat walked back to Whitney and sat down again. "Schoolteachers," he said. "We're getting NEA's support. Listen, this is an incredible organization we're fixing to build."

Whitney smiled.

Nat went over to Francy's typewriter. He took some bills from his wallet and gave them to her. She left.

Whitney began working on the printouts. She was almost at the end of the B's.

A while later, Francy returned with a huge McDonald's sack. She began handing out hamburgers. Whitney felt hungry. She took two hamburgers from Francy.

Francy sat at her typewriter and began working. Nat gave her a hamburger. "Eat, Francy, eat," he said.

"I'm on a diet," she said, pushing her glasses back up the ridge of her nose.

"Francy needs to see a doctor," one of the school-teachers said to Whitney, "if you know what I mean." The schoolteacher was wearing a football jersey and awful-looking shorts. She had a whistle around her neck.

"You teach P.E., huh?" Whitney asked her.

The woman blew her whistle softly. "And Biology. EPIC."

"I went there."

"Where do you go now?"

"School of Fine Arts."

"What area?"

"Drama."

"Very good, very good," the teacher said, distracted by something behind Whitney. Whitney glanced back. The TV set was on. Local news. Whitney worked on the last few names until the campaign story came on. The camera flashed to Albert Naylor, Cal's opponent in the race. It was the first time Whitney had gotten a look at him. He was at a barbecue or something. His wife was beside him and three children—younger than Whitney—were all over Naylor. "We are pro-life, pro-family, and pro-community," Naylor said and picked up one of his sons.

"Your dad will probably never put you on TV," Nat said.

Whitney looked at Nat.

"He's not the type to use his children like that."

"What does Naylor mean by pro-all those things?"

"Buzz words for anti-abortion, pornography, and public education."

Whitney went to the telephone and dialed home. Mary Ellen answered.

"Just wanted you to know I'm at headquarters," Whitney said.

"That's good of you, sweetie."

"It's O.K., here. It's really all right."

"Good. I'm happy it's a positive experience. Dad is on his way over there. I've got soup-line duty at the church, so don't count on me home until after eight. Tell Francy hi and that I love her."

"Bye," Whitney said. She went over to Francy's desk. "Mom says hi and she loves you," Whitney said. Francy had eaten the hamburger bun but not the meat. She was staring at it. "I love your mother," she said. When she looked up, her eyes were tearing.

"Francy," Nat said. "What is it?"

"I haven't eaten any meat in seven days."

"Watch out," Nat said. "Naylor's people believe vegetarianism is akin to secular humanism."

"I'll keep it quiet, Nathaniel," Francy said.

"Is that your real name?" Whitney asked him.

"I'm taking this to my puppy," Francy said and held up the hamburger meat. She almost cried again, but Cal came bursting in, and all eyes went his way. Whitney had never seen him so vibrant—face all aglow, wearing a bright scarf and new overcoat. He was like a movie star, only sober. Whitney felt something new— strong yet tender—inside. It was not that she'd always considered him boring, exactly, it was just that he was, first and foremost, her father, which implied a certain element of boredom. Secondly, he was a clergyman. He was, of necessity, restrained and languid, with a deep baritone voice. St. Francis of Assisi statues with birds lighting on fingertips reminded her of Cal, along with paintings of the Gentle Shepherd—His hand reaching to retrieve a lost animal. He was tall and, according to Whitney's friends, very handsome. He'd always been a clergyman, as far as Whitney knew. She didn't remember Ft. McClellan—they got her when she was an infant, then moved to Birmingham when she was two. The photographs were all the same—family snapshots of Cal, Mary Ellen, and Whitney—taken in gardens, parsonages, or churches, with Cal holding her, all smiles.

On Saturday morning, Francy came by to pick Whitney up. She sat in her dark-blue car, staring ahead, hypnotized by something.

Whitney got in.

"What's going on, Francy?"

Francy broke from the trance. "Ready to work?"

"You bet," Whitney said.

Francy reached onto the back seat and grabbed a handful of leaflets. "We have five thousand of these," she said.

"What are we going to do with them?"

"First, we're going to the Galleria. We have permission to distribute there—on the cars. Got on your walking shoes?"

Whitney glanced at her Reeboks. "Right," she said.

Francy kept pushing buttons on the radio as if searching for a particular song or news item. It was like Francy was always looking for something she couldn't find.

"Did you eat breakfast?" Whitney asked.

"That sounds like something your mother would ask me."

"Well, did you?"

"Cheese toast and kiwi fruit."

Francy pulled off her clip-on earrings and put them in the pocket of her oversized orange sweater.

"I like what you got on," Whitney said.

Francy was wearing the sweater over black stirrup pants with high-top sneakers. Whitney thought Francy was attractive, only she was, of course, too skinny.

The entrance to the Galleria was marked by fancy

ironwork that curled into the shape of two swans. Francy parked the car and laid out the strategy to Whitney. They would start at opposite sides of the parking lot and work toward the center, tucking "Calvin Gaines for Congress" leaflets under the windshield wipers. Whitney stuffed her bicycle pack full of leaflets and walked to the end of the parking lot. At first, it was awkward, leaning over the hood to secure the leaflets under the wipers, and she felt a bit uncomfortable, too, like she was invading everyone's privacy at best, or, at worst, committing a petty crime. Across the lot, she saw Francy's orange sweater and black pants, circling the cars, moving closer to the center where they'd eventually meet, task accomplished. Her uneasiness over what they were doing subsided, and she worked fast, developing a pace that was rhythmic and good. When she and Francy finally did come together, she looked at her watch. Almost two hours had passed. She'd experienced this when working on a play—getting lost in time. The strange part was why it felt good if you didn't even know it was happening until it was all over.

They walked back to Francy's car.

Francy got some cans of fruit juice from a cooler in the backseat. They sat on the hood of her car and drank it. A kind of Indian summer was lingering this year. Over the ridge, some trees had refused to shed all their leaves.

A woman approached Whitney and Francy. She was carrying a leaflet.

"Did you put this on my car?" she asked.

"Yes, we did," Francy said.

Whitney looked the woman over. She was wearing a fancy tennis outfit. She looked Mary Ellen's age.

"Well, you ought to be ashamed of yourselves."

Whitney and Francy didn't say anything.

The woman looked at Whitney. It was a severe look —the kind a teacher gives when you're caught in a bad act.

"You're too young to be doing this kind of thing. You don't know what you're asking for. This man is a danger to our children," she said, pointing to Cal's name. And then more gently, she added, "But you probably don't realize what's going on, do you?"

The woman walked off. Her legs were tanned. Whitney stared at her own Reeboks. This was not a feeling she liked—being scolded.

"Did you know that Naylor's people have tracked down every last detail about Cal's past, and Mary Ellen's past, and yours for that matter," Francy said, twisting her rings. "They know the place where you were born, near Ft. McClellan."

"How weird," Whitney said. She could tell Francy was getting too worked up. Generally, this meant she'd end up crying and not wanting to eat.

"Let's go, Francy," Whitney said. "Let's go get a pizza."

"I typed your father's sermon yesterday. He talks about the danger of a few people believing they've got all the answers. He says, 'Let's don't put each other down. God may call *you* to work to preserve the traditional family and, at the same moment, call *me* to fight for women's rights. Nobody's right and nobody's wrong. It's just a calling.' Listen, I can't eat a pizza because I'm not eating meat."

"We don't have to order meat. We'll get mushrooms and black olives."

"O.K.," Francy said.

They got into Francy's car and drove away. Whitney looked back at the parking lot. Cal's name clung to every car, but the leaflets were flapping precariously in the wind. Whitney wondered if they were secure enough under the windshields to keep from blowing away.

T H R E E

The sanctuary was in the shape of a dome so that the pale ivory walls sloped upward, gradually becoming a ceiling. Whitney had always felt it was like being inside a big eggshell. In more recent years, she'd imagined what a great theater-in-the-round the sanctuary would make if the straight-lined pews were placed in a circle, with Cal's pulpit center stage.

Cal began his sermon with a story about his grandfather in World War I. A comrade had jumped on a mortar and was blown to bits, sacrificing his body to absorb the explosive, thereby saving the life of Cal's grandfather and others who were nearby. Some of the signs Mary Ellen made for the deaf congregation during this opening story were spectacular, and Whitney watched the men and women closely, as they heard Cal's words with their eyes—fixed on Mary Ellen's hands. Mary Ellen was wearing a bright red dress and a black hat with a feather. She was one radiant cardinal, Whitney thought, recalling the offertory anthem's chorus: "This is my story, this is my song." The gist of Cal's vignette was that he, Cal, owed his life to this soldier—that, even before he, Cal, was born, a man had given his life so that Cal might eventually be conceived through his paternal ancestral line.

Whitney got lost in her own things, then, not wanting to, because she'd intended to hear this sermon that Francy had previewed for her while they were placing the literature on the cars the day before. But it was the part about Cal's lineage that caused her mind to wander. That—and what Francy had told her about Cal's opponent's knowing where Whitney was born and adopted near Ft. McClellan—was disturbing but also intriguing. It was the first time she'd ever felt any degree of curiosity about the whole matter. The soldier hadn't really given his life for *her* because she had not been, biologically speaking, in Cal's line. She imagined herself a solitary star, having burst into light from a dark nothing—kind of like the Big Bang Theory.

At the close of the service, three Hispanic families came forward during the invitational hymn. Mary Ellen, signing the lyrics to "I Surrender All," was almost crying, it appeared. Yet Whitney knew her mother wore this look most all the time—like her face was breaking. It was a big part of her beauty.

Cal introduced the new members. One family was from Guatemala, the other two from El Salvador. Then the "adoptive families," as they were called, came to the altar, too, and stood with them. Whitney knew that

somebody her age was probably now sharing a bedroom just as she'd done, grudgingly, with Maria.

The next day, the morning newspaper read: "Candidate's Church Harbors Illegal Aliens, Opponent
Charges." Cal smiled at the headline, unpeeling a soft-
boiled egg. Monday mornings always found him in a
relaxed state, no matter what, Whitney had observed.
She guessed maybe it was because Sunday was the big
work day, making Monday morning breakfast a kind of
Friday afternoon for preachers. Cal ate the egg along
with whole-wheat toast.

Mary Ellen had already left for her monthly Mothers
for Nuclear Disarmament breakfast meeting. Whitney
ate some raisin bran and scanned her reading assign-
ments for school. But she kept glancing at Cal. She
wanted to say something—she wasn't sure what.

"Francy and I gave out a lot of pamphlets Saturday."

Cal turned to her with a distracted smile. She knew
he was still lost in the newspaper article.

"We worked the parking lot at the Galleria."

He patted her hand. "We appreciate that."

"Some woman harassed us."

"Harassed you?"

"Gave us a hard time."

"How's that?"

Whitney shrugged. "Francy says the other side knows
all about us—you and Mom and me."

Cal smiled. "I can't imagine anything damaging coming up, can you?"

"No. We're pretty boring."

"I wouldn't say that."

"Where was I born?"

"Near Ft. McClellan. You know that, right? Have
known that?"

"Yes. But the place itself. Was it a hospital?"

"Well, yes, but we used to call these hospitals 'homes
for unwed mothers.' "

"Unwed mothers," she said and laughed.

"Pretty archaic, huh?"

"A euphemism? Is that a euphemism?"

"I suppose it was, back then."

"For being knocked up without a husband."

"Now, there are just 'single mothers,' right?" Cal noted.

"Yeah."

"So, am I hearing you say you are interested in your birth?"

"What all do you know?"

Cal put the newspaper aside. "No more than you do. But if you want to find out, I can check on what you need to do. Would you want me to do that today?"

"Sure."

Whitney gathered up her books and looked a long time at Cal's blue eyes. He was a good man, all right.

That evening, they sat in the kitchen eating supper. Whitney spooned potato salad onto her plate and watched the TV set. The local news was on. The anchorwoman began the campaign story, and Cal appeared on the screen. He was at a podium in the park. In the background were balloons, a hotdog stand, and autumn colors. Whitney didn't listen to what he was saying. She was looking at her mother on the TV screen. Mary Ellen wore a new sweater. It was white and looked like somebody had thrown red paint on it.

"Nice sweater, Mom."

"Thanks," Mary Ellen said.

After the election story ended, Cal flipped the TV off and pushed his plate aside. He hadn't eaten any chicken and had taken only a few bites of the salad.

"I'm sorry the TV's always on," he said.

Whitney saw that Mary Ellen hadn't eaten much, either, and now she sat at the table almost demurely in her colorful turtleneck, hands clasped, face alight.

Cal and Mary Ellen both looked sweetly at Whitney.

This was a look, an attitude, generally worn before a play of hers or after looking at a straight-A report card.

"What is it?" Whitney asked.

"Dad told me about your conversation this morning," Mary Ellen said. "I want you to know, sweetie, that we understand fully."

"Understand what, Mom?"

"Your interest in learning who you are."

"Oh."

Cal turned to Mary Ellen. "I believe Whitney already knows who she is," he said.

"Of course. But you know what I mean. I meant in a more concrete sense of the word. I realize she has a strong sense of identity. Certainly more than most women her age."

"More than most people *our* age," Cal noted.

"To be forty is to be fifteen again, according to Len Brodie," Mary Ellen said. Len Brodie was a pastoral counselor, a friend of her parents'.

"Hmm," Cal said, leaning back in a reflective, pastoral pose. "I'm not sure I fully agree with Len."

"You rarely agree with him," Mary Ellen said.

"That's not so," Cal argued.

Whitney watched, amused. She knew her father had no use for pastoral counselors. He believed ministers should be in the pulpit, in the community, in the *world* for that matter—feeding the masses, figuratively and literally. Mary Ellen, Whitney knew, believed in therapy.

"Do you see your Mom and me as being in the midst of an identity crisis?" Cal asked her, leaning forward. His eyes were like the blue in a fire.

"I think Len Brodie is having one," Whitney answered. It was an honest answer, she felt, recalling his new-wave wardrobe and rose-tinted glasses. Cal looked at Whitney, then at Mary Ellen, with a hint of triumph in his face.

"O.K., guys," Mary Ellen said, folding her hands demurely once again.

Cal took a tiny green spiral notebook from his shirt pocket. For as long as Whitney could recall, he'd carried one of these. In fact, there were drawers full of them—all colors—and a boxfull in the attic. He wrote sermons, kept financial records, journal entries, everything in these 3-by-5 pads.

He flipped over some pages and tore out a sheet.

"Here we are," he said, handing it to Whitney.

Cal's scribbling read: Hannah Home, Rt.4, Box 1, Anniston, Al. 555-8467. Contact person—Mae Ballard.

"You can call her whenever you like," Cal said, "and see what you need to do."

Mary Ellen smiled at Whitney once again—the "I'm-proud-of-you" look that Whitney found a bit puzzling for this situation, though she always welcomed approval for whatever reason. Then Mary Ellen turned back to Cal. "You can't tell me that you aren't just a little preoccupied with appearances these days. Just like when you were seventeen."

Cal threw his hands up. "Hey, I'm not arguing with anybody," he said.

"And *I'm* not pointing fingers. Look at me," she said, pointing to her new sweater—the one that looked like it had red paint thrown on it.

"You have to worry about how you look when you might be on TV at any moment, though," Whitney said. "I think it's just the campaign, Mom, not an identity crisis."

Whitney made the call on Friday, after school, from her bedroom, sitting on her rust-colored bedspread, staring at the giant poplar in the backyard. Mae Ballard herself answered the phone. "Hannah Home," she said. "Miss Ballard." Her voice caused Whitney to envision a long hall. There was a kind of echo. And Mae Ballard was apparently old. Her voice was husky. Whitney explained who she was, that she was "of age," and interested in her birth records. Miss Ballard said, "Hold, please," and after a while returned.

"You may make an appointment, Miss Gaines," she said and coughed.

Whitney was at a momentary loss but finally said, as confidently as possible, "I will be in the area next week. Friday? Three-thirty?"

"Let me check my book, Miss Gaines. Hold, please."

And, after another pause, her voice returned. "I will see you at that time." Then she told Whitney all the identification documents she would need.

Whitney thanked her and said goodbye.

Cal had planned to drive up with Whitney, but he had to man the Food Bank at the last moment when the designated church member got tied up at a luncheon honoring a poet from Nicaragua. Cal explained all this in great detail to Whitney over the phone, having called her at school, pulling her out of an art appreciation class. She was in the school office, listening to Cal's ramblings. He wanted her to read the Nicaraguan poet's work, he said, because it might make for a great interpretive reading for chapel. Nothing bored Whitney more than Central America—unless it was the thought of an interpretive reading. And anyway, her mind was already traveling the highway to Ft. McClellan.

"So listen, Dad. Is Francy around?"

"That's just what I was leading up to say. Yes, she is, and she's more than happy to leave here and drive up with you."

"Great. Tell her to come at one. I'll be on the front steps by the auditorium."

Francy pulled up at one sharp, in Cal's car. She was wearing the black stirrup pants from Saturday, but she had on a white churchy blouse with oval buttons and a navy-blue blazer—so that, from the waist up, at her desk, she probably looked her role as church secretary, Whitney thought.

She was drinking a Mountain Dew and eating popcorn.

"Here," she said, holding the brown paper bag over for Whitney to grab a handful.

"This was left over from the A.A. meeting last night," she said later. Whitney stopped munching momentarily. For a second, the thought of leftover A.A. popcorn was unappetizing, but it passed. The neighborhood A.A. group met in the church basement on Thursday nights.

"So what is this like for you?" Francy asked.

It was worded like a Mary Ellen question.

"It's not such a big deal probably. All I'll find out is some names—if I find out that much."

"What did Cal and Mary Ellen think about you wanting to know?"

"Not much."

"You're lucky, you know. They're unusual people."

"I know."

"Well, I've joined a group," Francy said.

"A group."

"A woman's group. It meets at the hospital actually. It's for women with eating disorders."

This was the first time Whitney had ever heard Francy label her problem. She didn't say anything, but nodded quietly—something Mary Ellen had taught her to do. Active listening, her mother called it.

"Part of my problem is my mother."

Whitney looked at Francy.

"All of us in the group have controlling mothers," she continued. "We are silently fighting their control."

"By not eating?"

"Yes."

Whitney turned to the window. There was something funny about that. She was glad she didn't have any disorders. She'd hate to have to join a group.

Francy exited off the freeway after another hour or so.

"Look in my purse," she said, "Get that little red notepad."

Whitney opened Francy's straw bag. Inside was a New Testament, nail polish, and what looked like a pocketknife but might have been just a fingernail-file. She got the red notepad out.

"Dad gave you this, didn't he?"

Francy smiled. "Of course. You know he's always got an extra one on him. Read me the directions."

Whitney read where to take each turn, and Francy drove on. They were on a country road.

"This is really in the boonies, isn't it?" Francy said.

They wound along, and the road narrowed under a canopy of autumn trees. They passed a Boy Scout camp and what appeared to be a church retreat site. Hannah Home was marked by a mailbox only—a big black one with white lettering. The Home was one large brick building, enclosed by a rather ominous fence.

"It reminds me of the Girls' School," Whitney said.

The Girls' School was for teenagers with drug problems. Actually, it was co-ed, but it used to be, according to Mary Ellen, the Girls' Reformatory, which accounted for the lingering gender emphasis. When Whitney was a child, she'd go there with her parents on holidays—bearing presents, food, and song.

Whitney and Francy went through the gate and up a few steps to the front entrance. The door was locked. Whitney rang a doorbell. Immediately—as if she'd been standing there anticipating the bell—an older woman, surely Mae Ballard, Whitney reasoned, appeared and said hoarsely to Francy, "Miss Gaines?"

"No," Whitney said. "I'm Whitney Gaines."

Mae Ballard stared then at Francy.

"I'm Francine Krueger."

"And you are what relation to Miss Gaines?"

"Her father's secretary."

"I see, I see."

Then Mae Ballard almost smiled.

When they got inside, Francy took a chair by the fireplace. "I'll wait here," she said. "I have a book to read."

"Yes. This is our parlor. Make yourself at home."

Whitney followed Mae Ballard down a corridor. Actually the interior reminded Whitney of her elementary school, so the pea-green walls, albeit boring, weren't foreboding. They went into a bleak office that had one large, wooden desk. On it was a solitary file.

Whitney handed Mae Ballard all the necessary identification that she'd been told to bring along. Mae Ballard studied it, then said, "You have contacted us just in the nick of time. We are closing this facility. Some of the records have already been sent to the State Department of Human Resources for microfilm and storing. Fortunately, yours was still here—the end of the alphabet. Zorn."

Whitney looked at her quizzically.

"Zorn. Your mother's last name."

A tingle of anticipation crept up on her, a feeling akin to excitement. And then she was overwhelmed by what was happening, a tad uncertain that she actually wanted the knowledge contained in the folder.

Mae Ballard glanced down at the identification documents again, her face suddenly changed.

"You're only eighteen," she said.

Whitney nodded.

"I'm sorry. The legal age here is twenty-one. I assumed you knew."

"I thought it was eighteen. So did my dad."

Mae Ballard shook her head. Then she looked inside the folder again.

"It's too bad," she said, "because your chart is flagged."

"What does that mean?"

"It means one of your birth parents has been looking for you. Just a minute."

She picked up the phone and dialed. "Holly," she said into the phone. "This is Mae. Check the computer for me, O.K.? Hannah Home, Ft. McClellan. Female. 5/10/66."

An eternity later, Mae Ballard said, "Thank you, Holly." Then she looked at Whitney. "It was your father," she said, "who was looking."

Whitney looked at her pleadingly.

"I'm sorry," Mae Ballard said. "It would be breaking a law if I showed you."

"I'm old enough to vote," Whitney said.

Mae Ballard looked at her for a long time. "This is your folder," she said. "I've got to leave the room for a few minutes. I'll be back shortly. You can wait here. You can sit behind my desk if you like." She looked at Whitney with intense and meaningful eye contact. Whitney felt confused. Mae Ballard closed the door. Whitney looked at the folder, and suddenly she understood. She knew what she was supposed to do. She knew she and Mae Ballard were above the law. She opened the chart.

It contained one report. And on the other side of the folder, an index card was stapled. It read "Face Sheet" and contained the following information:

> Name: *Diana Zorn*
> Birthdate: *3–20–48*
> Age: *18*
> Birthplace: *Mobile, Alabama*
> Eyes: *Blue*
> Hair: *Light brown*
> Weight: *Usual—112 lbs. At term—137*

Whitney jotted this all down in one of Cal's little notepads. Then she looked at the report. At the top of the page, it said, "Father: Sam Kirby." And it had an address: "c/o Eva Kirby, 3 Orchard Lane. Pineapple, Alabama." There was a phone number, too. Whitney reasoned that Eva Kirby must be Sam Kirby's mother. Her grandmother? It was a bit spooky. The report said that Diana was born to an "intact family," that her father was an attorney, her mother a housewife, that she had five siblings. She was a student at the University and hoped to complete her education after the adoption process was completed. She was studying theater—Whitney felt something inside when she read that. She felt, for a moment, like she might cry. The report went on to say that Diana was somewhat "affected" though "not histrionic." She did not appear depressed or distressed over her "situation" and felt no ambivalence over the pending birth and adoption. It was signed "Mae Ballard." So Mae Ballard had known Diana, her mother. That, too, was weird—just like everything else.

The call was made from Francy's apartment. To Whitney's surprise and relief, Francy had agreed to call the number of Eva Kirby—Sam's mother, they assumed—and identify herself as "an old friend from college, trying to get in touch with Sam." Whitney had feared that her own voice might sound too young, and Francy agreed. Francy warned her that the phone number on the report was eighteen years old and probably would yield no luck, but she'd be happy to try. Whitney felt a bit foolish, like she was thirteen again, having a friend call some guy for her while she listened in. But it had to be done. She was driven, now, to know more. Francy pulled her designer telephone into the sunroom. Whitney glanced over at the lovebirds. Francy had painted their cage purple.

"Hello," she said into the phone. "Ms. Kirby?"

Then she paused and gave Whitney the A-O.K. sign, making a circle with her thumb and finger.

"My name is Francine, and I'm an old friend of Sam's. Is there a way I can reach him?"

Francy jotted down a number, said "Right, yes, right," a few times, smiled, and then said goodbye.

"She was really nice," Francy said when she hung up.

Whitney looked at the number.

Francy pointed to the area code. "New York," she said.

By the time Francy got Whitney back home, it was nine-thirty. Cal and Mary Ellen weren't there. The note on the stove said: "At headquarters. Home by 10:00— give or take. Spaghetti in refrig. Love, Mom and Dad." It was Cal's scribbly handwriting.

Whitney told Francy thanks for everything. She went upstairs, sat on her bed, and dialed the strange number.

His voice, the hello, was alert and pleasant as if undisturbed by a late-night call. He said, yes, he was Sam Kirby. He didn't sound southern. "You don't know me," she began, then she told him the story—Hannah Home, Mae Ballard, the file, report, Eva Kirby's address and number. His responses were, at first, tentative, but gradually he warmed up—like he was studying the face of an old acquaintance, trying to recall, piecing it all together, until finally, "Yes! This is great!" And then he added, "I've been trying to find you."

They asked each other the kinds of questions you ask somebody you're getting to know. Whitney told him about Cal and Mary Ellen. She found out he was an artist, a cartoonist. She'd heard of the magazine where his things usually appeared. He was single. He had a roommate, Aaron. Eva was his mother.

"I found out about a computer network," he explained, "that matches up birth parents and their children. I gave them everything I could—my name, Diana's name, Ft. McClellan, May 1966."

"Yeah, the social worker told me you were looking. She called a woman named Holly who apparently had the computer in front of her."

"So your chart did get flagged. That's great. It's good to know that some systems work. Even in Alabama."

"Well, we break the law a lot in Alabama," Whitney said and told him about Mae Ballard leaving the room.

"Right. I was thinking the legal age there was twenty-one."

"Was Diana your girlfriend?"

"A friend."

"What color is her hair?"

"I think it was light red, blond?"

"Eyes?"

"Blue."

"And you. What color are your eyes?"

"Brown."

"Hair?"

"Brown."

"I guess I must look more like her."

"Well, what do you do? Do you have boyfriends?"

"Sometimes. I'm busy. School. Drama. I love acting. The report said Diana was studying theater. It said she was 'affected.'"

"Oh, I love it," he said. "I can't believe they let you read a psychological profile or whatever that was."

"Do you ever talk to her? Do you have her address?"

"I can probably get it and send it to you. I haven't seen her since before you were born. I went to the agency, once—the place where you were born."

"Spooky, isn't it?"

"I only saw it from the outside—that big, brick building."

"They're about to close it down. The social worker was the only one there the day I went."

"I drove up to see Diana a few weeks before you were born. She was real big, real pregnant. I felt bad. We talked through a fence. I remember that."

"My birthday's May tenth."

"I told Diana we ought to get married. We kept standing there at that fence. It was a chain-link fence. I'm sure I could have gone in, but we were the type to talk through a fence. Understand?"

"No."

"Dramatics. The fence was a prop maybe?"

"I understand props."

"Have you ever been in a situation where you know what you're saying has an unreal quality? Like a dream, maybe. Like you're getting high on fantasy?"

Whitney didn't know what to say.

"Have you ever had an affair?"

Whitney laughed. "An affair?"

"Have you ever messed around with someone else's boyfriend?"

"Yes."

"Thought you were in love?"

"Sort of."

"And the thing was, it was only the magic of knowing it wasn't yours, never could be, but you liked to talk like it could be?"

"When I was in that situation, we didn't talk much actually."

Sam laughed. "O.K., but you understand what I'm getting at? Have you ever had a day in your life when there was this big question of decision, and you knew you'd look back on it as a *big deal*, a crossroads, like, 'I'll remember this day the rest of my life.' "

"Yeah, I felt that way today."

"And it makes everything magnified and acute. Like the sky is *very* blue, and you're aware of it. Bird songs have a clear melody. Or the way somebody's hands feel —fleshy and bony at the same moment."

"That is hard to follow," Whitney said. This man has got to be a poet, she thought.

"O.K., back to acting. You know how it feels to be on stage?"

"Yes."

"Props. What was I saying about props?"

"The fence."

"Right. Diana and I were caught in a situation. But, at that moment, I thought, To hell with it all, let's get married, have this baby, and throw it all to the wind."

"Why didn't you?"

Sam said he didn't know. Whitney told him it was O.K. She said she'd write soon. He told her to please send a picture of herself. She said goodbye and went downstairs to wait on Mary Ellen so she could tell her everything.

FOUR

Eva had gradually come to understand that
she'd never have grandchildren—unless, of
course, there was a way for two men to adopt.
She and Sam hadn't actually acknowledged
things, but she had known ten years ago when
Sam first brought Aaron home to meet her.
My, but they are different, commented her
neighbors whenever they saw their photographs—framed, beside one another on her
piano. Sam, her son, was dark and muscular.
Aaron was angelic, light. In some ways, she was
closer to Aaron than to Sam, her son. That's

why, when Sam first called with news that he'd discovered he had a daughter from his relationship with Diana, back in college, Eva's heart went first to Aaron, fearful that he'd feel left out or strangely jealous.

They flew in from New York a week before Christmas. The flight was late. Eva went into the airport gift shop and selected some postcards for Aaron. He liked Alabama countryside and always wanted pieces of it to carry back North. He had grown up in New York. Then Eva browsed through the magazines, looking for Sam's cartoons. She was still amazed that he was appearing in magazines that most people had heard of.

Eva sat beside the gate designated for their arrival flight. This wasn't a busy airport, generally, but that night was a bit hectic—the holiday homecomings. All over the place were girls who looked eighteen, *her* age —the age of Eva's recently found grandchild. Actually, Eva had known, Sam had known, that he had indeed fathered a child way back years ago. It was in the days before abortion was safe—in their state, anyway—and what was the mother to do but go to a home for unwed mothers, have the baby, and place her in good, adoptive hands. Eva forgot, over the years. Sam said he forgot, too, though there are some lost things, Eva believed, that, once found, suddenly take on idyllic qualities, causing you to wonder, How did I ever live without?

The plane arrived. Eva stood at the window, watching it taxi in. The pane was cold. The airport lights ahead were pinpointed pinks and blues. Happiness. She felt it. For Eva, it crystallized into recognizable form only at unpredictable moments. It had nothing to do with anything. She found it isolated and random.

So here they came—all bundled up and northern-looking. Scarves, gloves, hats, the works. She hugged Sam first, then Aaron.

"How *are* you?" Sam asked, hooking an arm to hers.

"Just doing fine. You're O.K.?"

"Great."

"The flight?"

"Fine."

"How are *you?*" she asked Aaron. His cheeks, usually pale, had a bit of color—like a peach.

"Glad to be in the South," he said.

Aaron liked it here much better than Sam.

Eva gave them hot cider at home and brownies. They sat in the living room—Sam in the old brown recliner that had been his father's favorite. He was sprawled all over it like a big bearskin rug. Sam had begun working out with weights in high school and never quit.

"Great stuff, Mother," he said and bit into another homemade brownie. "I like them like this. Full of nuts."

"They're from Hazel's tree—the pecans."

"Hazel," Aaron said. "Next door. The one who has the beauty shop on her porch." He was on the piano bench, looking through sheet music.

"She had a girl working for her last fall. Do you remember the Yancey family?" Eva asked Sam.

"No, I don't."

"Yes, you do."

Sam took another brownie.

"They lived over on Cottage Hill," Eva continued. "You went to school with a Yancey girl. She had braids and was the first person we knew to wear braces. Anyway, it was her baby sister that went to work for Hazel —mostly shampoos but some cut-and-curls. She was pregnant with quintuplets, and, as Hazel put it, each and every one of them illegitimate. She lost all five in mid-trimester. It was awful. I felt so bad for her."

"What was the problem?" Aaron asked. "Why did she lose them?"

"I don't know."

"Can you imagine how that must have hurt?" Aaron said. Then he set some music up, turned on the piano lamp, and began a sonatina.

Sam reached in his wallet and pulled out a photograph. "Here she is," he said. "Whitney."

Eva felt it all over. She was Sam made into a girl—only her eyes were blue instead of brown. Her teeth were slightly miscast like Sam's—in that curious but not unattractive way, causing you to study her smile. Eva looked over at Sam. His face was bright. It was the look he'd worn as a kid, whenever he brought home something to show her—an animal he'd found, a cartoon he'd drawn, a handful of rocks.

"She wants to meet all of us eventually. She lives in Birmingham, you know."

"What do you want to have, Sam, when she comes? Chicken, fried chicken? Sweet potatoes? Beans? A pecan pie? A lemon-icebox pie?"

"Calm down, now. She's not coming any time soon. Food's not important, anyway."

"Well, it is, too."

Sam held the picture out, surveying it from all angles.

"Does she look like me?"

"You know she does."

Aaron's piano music abruptly changed course. The sonatina ended and he launched into a racing Beethoven rondo. Then he whirled around on the piano bench and faced Eva squarely.

"You know, my wife and I lost a child," he said, his eyes icy.

Eva knew he'd been married once. She didn't know anything else.

"No, I didn't know. I'm sorry."

"Death in utero. She was six months along. They made her carry it to term."

"I'm sorry."

"It was a boy."

"A son."

Aaron turned back to the piano, returning to the sonatinas, to his light handling of the keyboard. Sam got up and went over to Aaron. He began drawing imaginary pictures—random shapes and designs— with his finger, over Aaron's back. It occurred to Eva that, maybe, like his father, Sam had a hard time being gentle.

During the night, she got up. Sleep wasn't coming easily. She moved quietly down the hall. The old grand- father clock chimed twice. Light shone where the closed kitchen door met the floor. She opened it cau- tiously, knocking first.

"It's me in here," Aaron said.

He was on her wooden stool, leaning over the coun- tertop, looking at a photograph album. The stove's flu- orescent light cast a lavender tint over all the nearby objects—trivets, the sugar dish, Aaron's hands.

"Can't sleep?" Eva asked him.

"Never sleep my first night in Alabama. Jet lag. Cul- ture shock."

"What on earth is shocking here?"

"Nothing," he said and smiled. "Believe me, noth- ing." Then he added, "It's warmer."

"This floor is like ice," she said.

She turned on the space heater.

"I want to move here," he said, still looking over the old photographs. "I want to buy some land, a few acres, and move here."

"Well, you know my response to that."

"What's your response to that?"

"I'd be thrilled. Do you want some camomile tea?"

"Sam won't think of leaving New York."

"Tea?" Eva asked, putting on the water.

"Sure. Thanks."

"Sam won't come back," Aaron said. "He's got prob- lems with Alabama."

"There's no problem with Alabama. He's just got his own problems, don't you imagine, maybe?"

"Maybe."

"I like this picture," Eva said, pointing to a picture of

Sam, Sr., a black-and-white of him underneath an oak tree, smoking and trying to smile.

"Was he a good man?"

"He drank."

"I thought he was a preacher."

"He was."

"Sam says he was in bad shape there at the end."

"He went off the deep end, you know, over the edge. He was in a state hospital."

"Diagnosed?"

"He believed he was being persecuted."

"He probably was if he was at a state hospital."

"You're the social worker. You know more about all that than I do."

"Probably not. I rarely see schizophrenics. And anyway, going crazy in New York City is probably quite a different experience than going crazy in Alabama. Has Sam always been stubborn?"

"I was in labor with him thirty-six hours."

"That's dreadful."

"How is he doing these days?"

"He's practically famous, you know. All you have to do is open the right magazines."

"That's what I hear. That's what he tells me."

"And now he has his daughter."

"How are you with the thought of meeting her?"

Aaron shrugged, still staring at the picture of Sam, Sr., under the oak tree, smoking and trying to smile.

"So is he much like his father?" Aaron asked.

"I'm not sure."

"How did he kill himself?"

"He wired up his bed, grabbed the metal post, and did it that way."

The refrigerator made a noise. A neighborhood dog barked. Otherwise, all was quiet.

"You're not thinking of leaving him, are you?"

Aaron turned the page of the album to a shot of Sam, dated August 1955. Sam was hanging upside-

down on the bars of a jungle gym, grinning, a real
monkey. "No," Aaron said and smiled. "I'm not leaving
him."

Sunday rose, a light pink in the morning sky. Eva got
up, remarkably refreshed, and mixed up a batch of biscuits. At seven, Aaron walked back into the kitchen,
clad in a handsome, dark-blue suit.

"Heavens. What is this?"

"You're going to church, aren't you?" he asked, eyeing her bathrobe.

"Of course."

"I'm going, too."

"Well, by all means. Coffee?"

"Sure."

They baked the biscuits, then spread margarine inside all of them.

"What kind of jelly is this?" he asked, holding up a
jar of Hazel's canning.

"Crabapple."

"It's an interesting color," he said, looking closely at
the pale green.

"You've never had crabapple jelly?"

"No."

"Hazel canned it."

"Hazel who grew the pecans."

"Right. She has a crabapple tree, too."

"Sam's still asleep."

"Are you sure you want to go to church?"

"Absolutely."

"You're not just doing this as a have-to kind of favor
for your mother-in-law?"

"Mother-in-law," Aaron grinned, color rising in his
cheeks.

"Well."

Aaron drove Eva's old station wagon. He looked almost healthy in his Sunday suit. She knew that, if he'd

stay here a month, she could fatten him up and darken his wan face with southern sunlight. They pulled up in front of the chapel.

Inside, they took the back pew. The acolyte, a small boy, lit the candles. The service was beginning. Holiday poinsettias lined the altar, each given in memory of the dead by the living. Eva knew the one she'd chosen for Sam, Sr. It was a bit spindly but very red. It wasn't like the others. She didn't listen to the sermon. Instead, she began to plan what she'd do someday for her grandchild, Whitney.

FIVE

The phone cord stretched just enough to reach the old loveseat where Eva settled herself underneath the oil painting—a girl playing the harp. The sound of Aaron's voice was always a pleasant occurrence.

"Hello, Eva? Aaron."

"I was thinking of you this morning. I wish you could see the azaleas in my front yard. I'm looking at them right now."

"I thought they bloomed in April."

"They're early this year. Pray for nice March weather. A hard frost would do them in, especially these Pride of Mobiles."

"What?"

"It's a variety. A strong pink. How is Sam?"

Aaron cleared his throat. "O.K."

It was to the point where Eva knew Aaron like a son. Something was wrong, but she'd wait for him to begin. She surveyed the dogwood. It was, undoubtedly, the most handsome in the neighborhood. When it was quite young, the trunk had divided itself—decisively, at the base—so that the two main branches grew apart and held themselves wide and high like the arms of an orchestra conductor at the moment of crescendo. What this caused was a profuse spray of white blossoms that grew inward toward the center because, in essence, the tree's flowering was doubled.

"How are the neighbors?"

"Hazel's got a place over her left eyebrow. They're removing it Wednesday."

"A skin cancer?"

"I don't know. It's a bit dark."

"It always scares me to hear something like that."

Eva caught sight of some wisteria in Hazel's yard. It was only a light growth and hung delicately. Eva knew most people considered spring a new beginning. But, for her, its onset caused a feeling of wariness rather than hope. You never knew what might get nipped in the bud. In ways, she preferred the certainty of dead winter, its cold clarity.

"Eva?"

"I'm here."

"Listen, Sam wants to come home again in a few weeks."

"That's wonderful."

"Says he wants to see April in Alabama."

"How unlike him," she said.

Something must be wrong, Eva reasoned. They never came home more than once a year, and Sam wanting to see April in Alabama was just too much—considering his disdain for his southern heritage. She didn't care, though, if something was wrong. As long as nobody was dead or dying.

Eva hung up, after getting the flight number and arrival time. She went to the backyard and filled the birdfeeder with sunflower seeds. She had on her favorite sweatshirt. It was a bit too warm, but it was brown—the color of dirt—and she liked to wear it on gardening days. First, she got her hand-size shovel and went deep for the spring onion roots, tossing the pesky things into a trash bag for discard. Next she rearranged the bricks that had gotten all askew during winter, so that the garden border began to assume a kind of symmetry she liked. This made her want a cigarette, though. She debated it. She hated the things, as a habit, but allowed herself maybe one a season—at its onset—heralding the celebration.

She went over to Hazel's. Several years ago, Hazel had converted her porch to a beauty shop—a long, paneled business establishment on Orchard Lane. Eva knew that Hazel didn't charge enough, and she often gave free shampoos and sets "to charity" as she'd say, hauling in wayward girls from the reformatory, battered women from the church shelter, or just old graying widows surviving on their husbands' pensions. They'd sit by Hazel's pecan tree in lawn chairs, waiting their turn at the sink.

Today, there was only one woman in the shop. She was under the dryer. Hazel was doing her nails. Hazel glanced up when Eva walked in.

"Hey, love," Hazel said.

Eva looked directly at the dark, raised place over Hazel's eyebrow. "Sugar, don't worry," Hazel said. "They're taking it off on Wednesday." She massaged her customer's plump fingers gently. Hazel reminded Eva of Lucille Ball, something in her face.

Eva searched the countertop for a cigarette.

"What do you need, love?"

"A cigarette."

"Look in that cabinet."

Eva laid her hand shovel by the sink and opened the cabinet over it. The shelf was lined with hairspray, gel, and cartons of Pall Malls. She began tearing the cellophane.

"Take the whole pack," Hazel said.

"I just want one. I won't smoke another until September."

"Your habits are odd, my love."

Eva smiled and held the cigarette lightly in her palm. She got a pack of matches from Hazel, went back to her yard, sat on a big rock, and smoked. She studied the rectangular area she'd cleared for planting. In her mind, she imagined what it'd look like in July—the tomato plants bearing fruit, the bright marigolds, green peppers, a variety of herbs.

Over at Hazel's shop, the jalousie windows were opening. Eva knew this meant closing time. Hazel always ventilated the place in late afternoon, releasing a strange mixture of fumes—hairspray, nail polish remover, and stale cigarette smoke. The customer who'd been under the dryer getting manicured was leaving. Hazel swept bits of hair—belonging to the woman, Eva guessed—out the door, and the wind caught the strands up, dispersing them meaninglessly.

The news of Whitney's existence had caused a change in Eva. When trying to describe it to Sam, all she could come up with was, "This is what struggling plants must feel like when they get a dose of Triple 8."

"What's that?"

"8–8–8. It's fertilizer."

Sam smiled. "Great image. Woman being fertilized, arms flexing into balls of muscle like Popeye after eating the spinach. I'll have to use that."

"Seriously," she said.

Sam touched one of her fingers lightly. "Tell me."

"You know you're the same old person, but you feel more fruitful. Doesn't she make you feel that way?"

Sam looked away, staring off into Orchard Lane's dead end.

Eva knew she'd read Aaron's voice correctly over the phone. Something was wrong.

"He's obsessed with her father," Aaron told her later that evening, on this—their first day home.

Eva stopped grating the carrots for a moment. She and Aaron were at the kitchen table, making slaw. She looked at Aaron closely, waiting for more.

"He's a minister, you know."

Eva nodded.

"Sam's got it in his head that the man is some tyrant. Oh, not a tyrant, just part of the religious right. You know what I mean."

"The kind who wouldn't exactly understand you and Sam—your relationship?"

"That. But also other things."

"Like?"

"Just opposite ends of the political spectrum. Sam's probably as polarized as he imagines her father to be."

Eva lifted the grater and looked at the orange mound of carrot bits. "What do you think? Enough?"

"One more," Aaron said and handed her another carrot. He'd finished shredding the cabbage.

"Has she written Sam much since Christmas?"

"A few times."

"Do you read the letters?"

"Sure."

"So she talks a good deal about her father?"

"Never. Sam does, in his to her. I mean he asks her questions."

"Like?"

"About her childhood, what she was taught, if they were strict, was she allowed to think for herself. She never answers those questions. She just asks him things about Diana, which he never answers. In a way, it's sad and funny."

"Sometimes I want to write to her."

"So, why don't you?"

Eva shrugged. "I figure she's got enough new in her life without some old long-lost grandmother hounding her with correspondence."

"Eva."

"What?"

"Don't be so selfless. Write her if you need to."

Eva finished the last carrot and rested her arm on the table. Aaron dumped the grated bits into the cabbage. Eva spooned in some diced sweet pickles.

"What else do you usually put in slaw?" Aaron asked.

"That's it. Other than the mayonnaise."

"Want to try something different this time?"

"What?"

"What have you got in here?" Aaron asked and went to the refrigerator. He pulled open the chiller drawer and got out a zucchini, onion, and apple.

Eva eyed him suspiciously.

"It won't be slaw," she said.

Aaron smiled—his cherubic, best one. "Sure it will."

"The apple has got to go."

"O.K."

"The zucchini, too."

"No. The zucchini stays. Trust me." He cut up the onion and grated the zucchini. Then he went to her pantry and brought out a small jar of pimiento. He opened it and dumped the slices in. "Now," he said. "You have some oil and vinegar?"

Eva went to the refrigerator and got the mayonnaise jar. She set it firmly on the table in front of Aaron.

"No mayonnaise. Oil and vinegar."

It was a stand-off. Aaron looked at her, tilted his head to one side, and smiled affectionately. He might as well have been a seven-year-old boy. She gave in.

"Whatever you want," she said.

At dinner, she watched Sam spoon the colorful mixture onto his plate. He didn't bat an eye. He took a first bite, then a second. He never said a word. She reasoned that they just ate it like this up there, and it was nothing peculiar at all.

Sam got his first look at Cal a week later at a newsstand in Selma—the only stand that carried papers from other cities. He scanned *The Birmingham News*. In the metro section, there was an obscure story of District 6's congressional race. There were photographs of the opponents: Calvin Gaines and Albert Naylor.

He paid for the newspaper and went to the park, adjacent the library. He sat on a bench. It was a cool, clear day. First week of April. Sam knew, from his boyhood, that these crystal spring mornings were brief—that, almost overnight, Alabama would be unbearably hot. Today, though, the air was light, the colors incredibly soft. Gradually, he allowed his eyes to fall on the article and photograph. He began to see that Whitney's father was his—Sam's—own age, probably (judging from the article) quite tolerant, with political views not unlike his own. And the man was handsome. It was all unsettling. There were things Sam knew about himself. It was easier to hate than to love. Repulsion was more comfortable than attraction. He felt more at home with misery than he did with happiness.

He got up from the bench and tossed the newspaper in a receptacle with a sign that read, "Keep Alabama Beautiful." He crossed the park, got in his car, and drove away from the city toward his mother's house in the neighboring county.

When he was a boy, the drive up to Selma was long and, in summer, arduous—in his father's old Ford. His parents only came here for special occasions—to take Sam to a Walt Disney film at the theater, to attend a multi-county revival at the city auditorium, to Christmas shop. And then, when Sam was in high school, he and his mother began bringing his father in to see psychiatrists. Sam knew his father was slipping long before anyone else seemed to notice. When discussing his father's illness later with a psychiatrist friend, he'd been reminded that, "It's hard to recognize the onset of grandiose religiosity when it's a minister, of course." Which was probably true. He remembered that the last sermons his father preached to his country chapel congregation were, according to some of the deacons, "true to the word of God." Never mind that his identification with Jesus had clearly exceeded its boundary and that he was talking about his, Sam, Sr.'s, own death as Easter season approached. He had wired up his bed on Good Friday, of course.

Sam, himself, had no use for religion.

The Interstate now connected the city to the small outlying town where Eva lived, but Sam decided to take the old backroads. Wild honeysuckle and kudzu were hungrily taking over the countryside, but the scattered neighborhoods along the way had well-manicured lawns with bright azaleas.

Sam crossed the county line and took Mineral Springs Road. He turned onto Orchard Lane, the dead-end street where his mother lived. He pulled in to the gravel driveway and saw Aaron and his mother in the backyard, sitting in green-and-white folding lawn chairs. Aaron's legs were outstretched, and Sam saw that his feet were bare in the cool, spring grass. He wore jeans and a T-shirt the color of orange sherbet. His hair was flaxen in the sun. Aaron's placid nature was foreign to Sam. He didn't actually envy it, he merely did not understand why some people, like Aaron, found life so sweet. He knew, for instance, that Aaron was, at this very moment, reveling in the way the Alabama sun felt on his skin, that he considered this and all conversation with Eva rich and meaningful, that the taste of this morning's spiced tea was probably still lingering in his mind.

Eva waved to Sam.

"Join us," she hailed.

"I need coffee," he called back.

He went inside, took the hot-water kettle from the stove, and made himself a cup of instant.

The screen door made its usual rusty noise, and Sam turned. Aaron's face was pink.

"You're already sunburned," Sam warned.

They sat at Eva's old wooden table. Sam spotted the indentations where he'd etched a drawing with a ball-point pen as a kid. The table had been brand-new at the time. His father had been furious.

"I did this," he said to Aaron, pointing to the etching.

Aaron smiled. "Budding artists can't control themselves. They do it everywhere they find a surface, right?"

"What have you and Mother been talking about?"

"Varieties of banana peppers."

"Interesting."

"Natural ways to get rid of aphids."

"Stimulating."

"Early Girl tomatoes versus Atkinson and Big Boys. Where did you go?"

"I drove to Selma."

"Nice drive?"

"It's a good time of year here. Azaleas are dazzling."

"Yeah. Eva and I took a walk."

Sam looked at his hands. "I found a Birmingham paper."

"Good. And was Whitney on the front page?"

"No." Sam smiled and examined his childhood drawing on the table. "But there was an article about her father, about the congressional race. There was a picture of him, too."

"So where is it?"

"I threw it away."

"Well, what did it say?"

"I had him pegged wrong. For one thing, he's our age. And he's part of the religious left, not the right."

"That's good news, isn't it?" Aaron asked.

Sam got up and poured the last of his instant coffee into the sink. Out the window, he saw Eva and Hazel idly pulling up weeds.

"I don't buy it," Sam said.

"Buy what?"

"It's all the same. They're really all alike. Same mold. No matter what his politics may be, you can't tell me he wouldn't go nuts over his daughter having a father with a mate named Aaron."

"You don't know that. He's probably very tolerant."

"You know, I hate words like 'tolerant.'"

Aaron's blue eyes wavered, looked away. Sam felt immediate regret and affection. "Let's take a drive this afternoon," he said. "Look at some land we'll be buying for you soon."

"You're patronizing me."

"I need to get my mind on other things, don't you think?"

"That's for damn sure."

"I'll get Hazel's Sunday paper and we'll check out real estate. Maybe there's a few acres nearby. We'll plan to close on our land by summer, O.K.?"

Aaron gave him a look. Sam knew that nothing would make Aaron happier than for him, Sam, to be serious about that. For a moment, he almost was—or wished he could be.

Eva understood that Sam's ever moving back home, to Alabama, had a highly remote chance of ever happening. Such a move would probably be preceded by the resolution of a multiplicity of old conflicts—or at least would herald the onset of such untanglings. She knew this partly from conversation with Aaron but mostly because Sam was her son. She wasn't exactly certain what the components of his resentment were. There were the obvious bad memories—growing up when he did, the Civil Rights Movement here, the rural mind-set of their community, his father's illness and death, and his ultimate conclusion that the church was responsible for all injustice he'd experienced or witnessed—personally and globally. But she believed that Sam's disposition was basically a problem of genetics— that he was, like Sam, Sr., destined from the beginning to be gloomy. Whether or not his or anyone else's dark side could be changed into light was, to Eva, the basic spiritual question. She wanted to believe the answer was yes, and she did believe it most days.

Like today. Eva and Hazel knelt close to the garden as they spaded up spring weeds. They had the necessary knee calluses of country women that permitted this kind of work to be done wearing shorts. Neither wore gardening gloves and neither was afflicted with arthritic hands. Their strong fingers worked like machine parts, prying the weeds up. Sam and Aaron had just left to take their drive to look at land.

"I'm hiring a new girl Monday," Hazel said. She lit a cigarette, held it in her left hand, and continued to weed with her right.

"I hope she works out for you," Eva said.

"Umm." Hazel drew on her cigarette. "She used to do shampoos and sets at the Curl Up and Dye."

"Experienced, huh?"

"That's right, love, and believe me, it counts."

Hazel put her shovel down and made a gesture of fluffing her curls, but actually her strawberry-blond, dyed hair was sprayed so stiff it was one big, unmovable mass. Hazel dyed her hair various colors. She said it was a way to display new products to her "ladies"— which was how she referred to customers.

"It's not the experience of setting hair that's so important," Hazel continued. "It's the knack of hearing all the ladies' problems, appearing to listen but minding what you're doing with their hair—as well you should be. And not getting involved. And," Hazel took a long scorching draw from her cigarette, "not gossiping. You can imagine."

Hazel flipped her cigarette into her own yard. "Those bluejays," she said. Eva looked up at Hazel's birdfeeder. The sparrows and goldfinch were scattering as a bluejay flapped madly then landed on the ledge. Sunflower seeds fell to the ground.

"There's a pecking order to everything," Eva noted.

"Yes, love."

The neighborhood was perfectly quiet. Eva stopped weeding, watching the goldfinch on the telephone wire, perched, waiting for the bluejay to move on. The sun was almost directly overhead. She eyed the raised, dark place over Hazel's eyebrow.

"We need to start wearing hats," Eva said.

Hazel waved it away. "We don't need protection against the elements. We've lived this long."

Eva stared blatantly at Hazel's eyebrow.

"The appointment's Wednesday, hon."

"I'm buying us some visors tomorrow."

Hazel looked over Eva's head. "You need a shampoo and set, my love. Come on—while your boys are gone."

Inside Hazel's old porch—her shop—Eva let herself unwind. She sank into Hazel's red vinyl wash-chair and leaned back so her neck rested on the sink's edge. Hazel cradled her head in one palm and squirted pink shampoo into Eva's hair. She washed it, then massaged Eva's neck. Eva looked up at Hazel's Lucille Ball face. The cobalt-blue eyes were intense—working on Eva's scalp and neck like an artist with clay. Eva loved Hazel, and suddenly the desire to speak of Whitney overcame her.

"I've not told anyone this," Eva said, feeling like one of Hazel's "ladies," desperate for a confidante.

"What, hon?" Hazel's hands stopped momentarily.

"I have a granddaughter."

Hazel's eyes widened, but she turned on the water-sprayer and began rinsing. Eva guessed this was what Hazel meant earlier about the importance of experienced hairdressers who appear to listen but mind what they're doing to the ladies' hair. She knew this was certainly startling news to Hazel, just as it had been to her, but Hazel kept on rinsing, then applied the conditioner.

"Sam had a girlfriend in college. Diana."

"I remember her," Hazel said. "A blond. Not a trace of a curl. She came over once when Sam had her at your place for dinner. Kind of a hippy-type, no?" Then Hazel wrapped a towel over Eva's hair and sat her upright from the sink. She sat down on a stool, lit a cigarette, smiled, then laughed. "A grandchild! Eva, that's news. A little granddaughter."

"Hazel, she's almost grown."

"Oh."

"Sam was in college a long time ago."

"Yes, you're right. Never mind she's grown—it's still news, she's still your grandbaby."

Eva wanted a cigarette bad, but she'd already had her ritual, seasonal smoke for spring. It'd have to wait for summer. Habits, Eva knew, were best kept intact.

"She's been with Diana all this time? Diana didn't tell Sam till now?"

"She was adopted. She got her records back in the fall and contacted Sam."

"Well, I'll be. I'll just be."

"It's a nice feeling, Hae."

"Sure it is, love."

"I mean I never thought there could be any."

Hazel patted her hand. "I know, love."

"I don't expect to establish a relationship with her." Eva laughed. "You know, I stopped expecting anything from life long ago."

"The only way to live, hon."

Eva peered through Hazel's opened jalousie windows. "Makes small things into big pleasures when you don't expect much. Like those Early Girls making from seed—hardiest plants I've ever grown. Anyway, I don't expect anything from her. It's enough to know she exists."

S I X

Whitney sat behind the front desk at head-quarters. It was almost dusk, late May. A long window ran the length of the building, giving her a view of Five Points—old bars, a dilapi-dated cafe, new neon party shops; in general, most structures were either in a state of disre-pair or newly repaired. The neighborhood was like a half-cleaned child's room—old toys, new ones in mild disarray. Cal's church stood in the heart of it all—the old Spanish design un-changed. She was alone. Nat and Francy had gone out for an early supper. The initial excitement of the campaign—back in November when Cal had announced—had waned just as Nat had said it would. He'd told Cal it was quite predictable, that spring and early summer would be the time for hard work, that he'd probably find the absence of media hype a relief, and that in September the news coverage, balloons, and general campaign frenzy would return of their own accord. In December, Cal had officially named Nat as campaign manager.

Whitney had since learned that Nat's grandfather had been a Congressman. Nat's father was a judge. One of the schoolteachers had told Whitney, "Nat's one of those guys who probably was destined to go to law school or something but makes this conscious decision to be a blue-collar worker instead." Whitney wasn't sure exactly what she meant by this. "But believe me, honey," the schoolteacher added, "they make more than we do."

Whitney saw a few people walk by. They passed, then turned back, peered into the window, and finally opened the door to headquarters.

"Hola," one of the women said.

They were Hispanic.

"Buenos tardes," Whitney replied, hoping they knew English. The woman who had spoken stood near the desk where Whitney sat. She had dark, friendly eyes and wore a huge skirt that looked more like a colorful tapestry than a garment. The other two—a man and a woman, a good bit younger—kept their distance.

"I am Rosa," the tapestry woman said.

"I'm Whitney."

"Yes. You are Whitney."

"Right." Whitney looked at her.

"I am a member in the church."

"Oh. O.K." Whitney gave her a Sunday smile.

"My friends," she said and extended her arm in a sweeping gesture of introduction, "Mita and Carlos."

Mita and Carlos looked at her timidly. Whitney gave

them a variation of the Sunday smile. In the Sunday smile, you let your face open so that the light flows. You want people to have the sensation of heavenly sunshine—teeth and all. For Mita and Carlos, she did most of it, but parted her lips only slightly, thereby creating a shy look of warmth. She didn't want to overwhelm them. She sensed their fear.

"We want to help with..." Rosa looked around the room for the word. She pointed to a "Calvin Gaines for Congress" poster. "With this."

"O.K." Whitney said. She got up. She had no idea what to put them to work on. Clearly, Mita and Carlos couldn't do phone canvassing, and she didn't know where the material was anyway. "I like your skirt," Whitney told Rosa.

"You want it? I give it to you."

"Oh, no. Thank you. But no."

It was one thing she'd noticed about these people— they were always wanting to give you something—even when they had hardly anything at all. Maybe that's why Cal and Mary Ellen liked them so much, Whitney thought. They were real stewards.

Whitney saw Nat and Francy crossing the street, and she was relieved. They'd know what to assign these people. Francy breezed in, all smiles, wearing a melon-colored spring dress. Since she'd joined the Eating Disorders group, she was happier; though, in Whitney's eye, she hadn't gained any weight yet. Nat began unloading something from the car parked by headquarters. Whitney started to introduce Francy to Rosa and her friends, but Francy and Rosa hugged each other before she had a chance.

"Como esta, Rosa?" she said.

"Bien. Bien."

Of course Francy knew them. She knew everyone in the church but especially the Hispanic families. Whitney knew that Francy handled a lot of whatever had to be done to get the families settled.

Francy took Mita's frail, dark hand, then Carlos's. She said a Spanish word Whitney didn't understand. Nat came in with a box full of new pamphlets. Francy introduced Nat to Rosa, Mita, and Carlos. He tipped an imaginary hat—a gesture Whitney thought odd. Francy took a stack of pamphlets from the box. "These look great, Nathaniel. The royal blue is perfect."

"We want to help," Rosa said.

"That's very generous of you. Here," Francy said, handing her some pamphlets. "If you don't mind going into a bar, hand some of these out over there, across the street." She pointed to Pharo's. "Nice people go there."

Nat disappeared behind the partition that led to the water cooler and storeroom. Francy continued her instructions to Rosa—how to work the neighborhood establishments without offending anyone. "They'll be receptive, especially if they've had a few."

Rosa nodded, but Whitney could tell by her expression she didn't know what Francy was talking about. Still, she accepted the pamphlets Francy was handing her, and she left with Mita and Carlos, chattering in Spanish. Whitney watched them cross the street, Rosa's rainbow skirt bold and bright even in the dimly lit dusk. They disappeared into Pharo's.

Nat called from the storeroom in back. "Francy!" It was like an alarm. Whitney and Francy hurried to the back. The storeroom was used by the dentist and attorney who rented the building. There were reams of stationery with the attorney's name, a Xerox machine, and an old dentist's chair—where Nat now sat, leaning over, face in his hands.

"What is it?" Francy asked him, moving closer.

He looked up. His face was red. "Have you *lost your mind?*" he said to Francy.

"No, have you?" she said, eyeing the dentist's chair.

He got up.

"You can't let those people do that."

"What people? Do what?"

"Those Latin Americans."

"Nat," Francy said softly, as if hurt. "They are members of our church."

"O.K.," he said quietly. He took her hands in his and faced her like a lover might. He was a real smoothie, Whitney thought. She liked his act even though it needed polish.

"Let's talk," he said, and all three of them went back to the big campaign room. This was an occasion when Francy might have cried, Whitney thought, in the old days before she began going to her group. Francy sat in a folding chair and crossed her legs, ladylike, at the ankle. She looked like a model in her melon-colored spring dress.

"O.K., Nat. So what's your problem?"

He raised an eyebrow.

Francy raised one back.

Squaring off. Whitney loved a good debate. She sat down on the desk top, a spectator. Nat rolled up the sleeves of his army-green work shirt, then jammed his hands into the pockets of his tight jeans. She imagined he was flexing certain muscles underneath his clothes, though none were visible.

"What's *my* problem, huh?" he said to Francy.

"Sit down, for God's sake," she said.

He pulled a chair up beside her. "My problem is that I'm responsible for making this campaign work, to make Cal win. There are some things you have to avoid. Generally speaking, people will elect the man— or woman—closest to the middle. The *moderate* as you all say in your church dilemma. Appearances matter. You can't send these Central American church members into a bar to campaign. It would be more prudent to use them here, at headquarters, kind of behind the scenes."

"I don't think Cal would agree with you."

"Listen, the point is that we shouldn't do anything to

rock the boat. Naylor is obviously way too far to the right to be electable. Cal *is* moderate, is in the middle. But there are some things he's involved with—as a Christian, I understand, not as a politician—that present the image of being left."

"You need to talk this over with Cal."

"Stop saying that! Stop being a damn secretary. What do *you* think? Don't you agree?"

Francy shrugged.

"I understand your sentiments about these people," Nat said.

"Sentiments." She stood up. "What a word, what a stupid word. We aren't sitting around, you know, intellectualizing about the situation in Central America. We are doing God's work."

Nat got up in her face. "The Sanctuary Movement is too emotionally charged, Francy, to flaunt in bars."

Francy sat back down and crossed her ankles. "Talk to Cal about it," she said.

"I really wish you'd stop saying that."

"Well, who's in charge—you or him?"

Nat ran his hand over his dark curls. "It's my job to steer the campaign. This is a matter of dodging an obstacle."

"What's the obstacle here, Nat?"

"Obstruction might be a better word, a potential obstruction."

"What's the obstruction?"

"What have we been discussing?"

"You view people as obstructions?"

"Your sentiments are getting in the way again. It's the *issue,* Francy, not the people. The issue, the obstacle, can throw us off course. You've seen it happen in other campaigns. A candidacy destroyed by one incident, one issue."

"Cal's not going to sacrifice his principles to win. He feels very strongly about this. So does Mary Ellen. Don't they, Whitney?"

Whitney didn't say anything.

"We'll talk about it," Nat said. "We'll all get with each other and talk it over."

Whitney told them goodbye and got on her bicycle. She pedaled leisurely and looked up at the stars overhead. The sky was a dome just like her father's sanctuary, only dark-blue instead of ivory. She parked her bicycle on the screened-in front porch and went inside. Mary Ellen was cooking in the wok. Whitney looked at the chopped vegetables and got a few of the raw cashews her mother was dumping into the sizzling oil.

"Hi there," Mary Ellen said. She signed this with one hand. Often, she signed unconsciously to Cal and Whitney as she talked.

"I've been at headquarters," Whitney said. She almost said something about Francy and Nat's disagreement, but one thing she was taught early on, as a minister's daughter, Don't say anything about what you overhear.

"You have some mail," Mary Ellen said.

Whitney looked in the straw basket where they always tossed the day's mail. The letter was from Sam, and it was postmarked Pineapple, Alabama, instead of New York. He was visiting his mother. Whitney went in the den and said hello to Cal, who was reading a newspaper. She glanced over his shoulder. The words were all Spanish.

"What's that?" she asked.

"*El Diario de Hoy.* It's a newspaper from El Salvador."

"Oh."

She sat on the couch next to him and opened the letter. It was short. Sam said he'd be in Alabama for a few weeks and maybe they could meet each other if she was "ready for that"—if not, he'd stay in touch. Then he told her he liked being South in spring and described his mother's neighborhood. It sounded like a nice place.

Whitney read the letter a few more times, then handed it to Cal.

"It's from Sam," she said.

Cal read it and smiled his pastoral smile.

"Well, are you going to meet him?" he asked.

"I don't know."

"Are you uneasy about it?"

"Sort of."

What she was uneasy about was him, Cal. She didn't know how to put it, but it had something to do with betrayal—like, if she met her birth father, she'd somehow be negating Cal's place as her real father, which indeed he was. In this sense, she was glad, relieved, that Diana had not answered her letters, because she had avoided this same dilemma with Mary Ellen. Sometimes she was sorry she'd ever read her records. If Cal felt in any way displaced or angry or hurt by her interest in Sam, she was certain he'd never say so—for fear of standing in the way of what she needed to do.

Nat came over after dinner. Whitney was at the kitchen table composing a letter to Sam when he arrived. To avoid dealing with Sam's question about their meeting, she was describing the interior of her father's church—the sanctuary dome and how she felt pedaling home under the stars. She knew it was a crazy thing to write about, but most of their letters were descriptions of surroundings. Sometimes it felt like a correspondence course in English composition.

She heard the doorbell, then the sound of Nat's voice.

"I'll get the coffee," she heard Mary Ellen say, and a second later, Mary Ellen was there, in the kitchen, where she began grinding dark Guatemalan coffee beans.

"Nat's here," Mary Ellen said.

"Yeah, I heard his voice."

"Studying?"

"No. I'm writing to Sam." She handed her mother Sam's letter. Mary Ellen read it and handed it back, giving her that puzzling, "We're-proud-of-you" look. She bent to kiss Whitney's forehead, and the hand-painted cross necklalce Maria had given her dangled from her neck.

"When you finish, you can join us in the living room if you like."

Curious about what Nat's tactic with Cal would be, she got up and followed her mother. Their living room was painted a vanilla color, and the walls were covered with colorful Central American tapestries and Indian art. Cal and Nat sat in matching rattan chairs. Both leaned forward toward the coffee table, the way men do when there's business at hand. Whitney curled up on the couch and began peeling her coral nail polish.

"Sorry to barge in like this, unannounced," Nat said. He'd apparently been home since leaving head-quarters, Whitney noted, because he was wearing khaki pants with an ironed crease rather than jeans. The khakis looked starched, like he'd just picked them up at the cleaners—which he probably had. He wore a baby-blue shirt with a button-down collar. Whitney had ob-served that Nat had an altogether opposite wardrobe from his usual steelworker garb that he wore on special occasions, generally when "off duty" from the cam-paign. At headquarters and for cameras, you could count on the steelworker look. Once, she mentioned this to Francy, who told her, "Unemployed steel-workers—a big issue here, a lot of votes. He probably wants to be a reminder."

Mary Ellen brought in two mugs—one for her, one for Nat. He smiled big. They loved coffee. Cal didn't drink it.

Nat inhaled the steam. "Smells great," he said.

"It *is* great," Mary Ellen told him. "It's from Guate-mala. One of our new church members gave it to us."

Nat glanced over at Whitney.

Whitney suppressed a smile.

Sometimes this whole deal—the campaign—was like a movie. She had no part; she was a one-man audience, and she found a good bit of it amusing. It reminded her of the conference in New Orleans a couple of summers ago—people being so serious over the issues. Most of life had been this way, the feeling of detachment, and she wondered if it was simply a symptom of being a minister's daughter. She knew she was a loner, that her friends were few, that she'd never been in love. She felt more alive on stage than in real life. She depended on acting for this reason, and she knew she was the best drama student in her school. She took it seriously just like these people took the campaign seriously. Cal and Mary Ellen seemed capable of being *involved* so easily. She wasn't this way. It made her wonder about Diana, her birth mother. Was she this way? An observer only? Was Sam? Were they so uninvolved with life, with each other, with their child, that Diana, as the report had said, "felt no ambivalence at all" about the pending birth and adoption?

It wasn't that she had no feelings—her mother's favorite word. She loved Cal and Mary Ellen immensely. She loved Francy. It's just that she dwelt in another sphere. The first time she kissed anyone passionately, she kept her eyes open, fascinated by the maze of tiny blood vessels visible under the closed eyelids of the guy. Church, of course, was an ideal spectator sport—and maybe that was, indeed, the source of it all. Being in the sanctuary that often, growing up, meant learning to study people and details—in order to bide time. The good thing—and this had happened only very recently —was that life no longer bored her so much. Being estranged but interested was certainly better than being bored and cut off.

Nat set his mug on the coaster and leaned forward

again, serious. He angled his body to Cal's.

"I wanted to talk with you about how we want to prioritize the use of volunteers during the summer. Phone canvassing or door-to-door or working the malls and neighborhood establishments."

Nat blew gently into his hot coffee, and the steam arose and dissipated.

Cal said, "You're the boss. Whatever you think."

"We're getting new volunteers."

"Great."

"Some of your church members came by this afternoon. Rosa," Nat raised his eyes to Cal, "Mita, and Carlos."

Cal smiled. "Rosa," he said, thoughtfully.

Nat glanced at Whitney again.

Whitney looked at her nails.

"They're with the Linton family," Mary Ellen said.

Nat raised his eyebrows and nodded, as if interested.

"I believe that Mita and Carlos are Rosa's cousins," Mary Ellen added.

Nat's big hands circled his mug.

"They have *some* story to tell."

Whitney hoped that Mary Ellen wasn't about to tell it.

Nat nodded, listening. Whitney looked at Nat's shoes. They had a dark wine tint and appeared freshly polished.

"Well," Nat said and looked around the room. His eyes came to rest on the hand-woven rug under his feet. "They are eager to help with the campaign."

"They adore Cal," Mary Ellen said. "They all do."

Nat stared at the rug.

"So we can probably count on the others, too," Mary Ellen said.

"The others," Nat said. "The other refugees."

"Yes," Mary Ellen said. "But they don't like that word. I'm not sure what it implies for them, but they prefer 'neighbors' or 'friends' or simply 'Salvadorans,'

'Guatemalans,' 'Nicaraguans'—depending on their country." She signed "neighbors" and "friends" as if Nat needed further interpretation.

"The new fliers are at headquarters. They look good. Francy had Rosa and Carlos and Mita distribute some over at Pharo's."

Cal leaned back, smiling. "That must have been some kind of experience for them."

"Yes. I was concerned."

"About the bar?"

Nat ran his hand through his hair.

"About Rosa and her friends being there in a bar."

"Nat," Mary Ellen said, leaning toward him. Her bronze knees were pressed together. She had on tropical-looking shorts. "Do you have some negative feelings about them?"

Nat smiled warmly. "Is that a nice way of asking if I'm prejudiced?"

"It would be if it were not in context of the campaign."

"You understand my dilemma, don't you?"

By now, Whitney noticed, they were all huddled quite close around the coffee table, all leaning forward, faces bright, a bit flushed.

Mary Ellen looked Nat in the eye. "Of course."

"I wish Francy were here," Nat said.

Mary Ellen leaned back, nodding. Whitney knew she was switching into "active listening."

"We didn't see eye-to-eye on this."

Mary Ellen drank her coffee.

"We had a disagreement."

Nat looked at Mary Ellen, waiting, Whitney supposed, for her to say something.

"I hope there weren't any hurt feelings," Nat continued.

Nat tilted his head and looked questioningly at Mary Ellen.

"She seemed to feel that there was nothing wrong

with Rosa and her cousins campaigning at Pharo's. I, on the other hand, had some reservations."

He stared at Mary Ellen.

"Go ahead," she said and signed this.

"That's about all there was to it, really."

"No hurt feelings, then," Mary Ellen said.

"No."

Mary Ellen set her empty mug on the table.

"But that still doesn't solve the dilemma," Nat said.

"No?"

"Well, what do *you* think?" he asked her.

"About?"

"About Rosa handing out leaflets in Pharo's."

"I can understand Francy wanting to give them this opportunity."

"Yes, of course."

He turned to Cal. "And, in the future, do you want them to continue to do this kind of work?"

Cal held his hands palms up. "I don't see what it would hurt."

Nat's face was red. His dark eyes were a bit wild. Whitney imagined him exploding.

"Sometimes at the end of a campaign, you can look back and know, 'This is where we lost the race.' I've been in that situation before. I don't want *this* to be such a juncture. I understand what you are doing as a minister, politics aside, and, believe me, part of your attraction is your ministry, your, ah, lifestyle, the whole 'urban dream,' but I'm telling you Naylor and his people will run with this Sanctuary Movement thing. You have to remember that this remains a conservative district. Don't kid yourself that everyone in this city shares the sentiments of those in your congregation. You've somehow managed to assemble quite a unique body there, or maybe you've changed their attitudes over the years, I don't know, but they are *not* a microcosm of District 6."

Cal stared at the rug, nodding.

Mary Ellen nodded, too.

It was clear that Rosa and her friends would, from now on, be in the storeroom, stuffing envelopes or stapling papers or counting names.

Whitney sat on her rust-colored bedspread and surveyed the room. She was still working on the letter to Sam. It was almost midnight. Nat had left on good terms with Cal and Mary Ellen. He'd smiled broadly after the conversation mellowed into small-talk and told them he'd better move on, that he had a date. Whitney took this in with interest. She felt a great degree of curiosity over the kind of woman Nat might like. She got up and went over to the full-length mirror attached to her closet door. She was wearing khakis, not unlike those Nat had on. Her shirt was white and unadorned, worn loose, like a kind of medical uniform. It was as if, in recent months, she had swapped attire with her parents. They'd given up the safari look and wore bright colors. She had laid off the turquoise-jams-look and was more into subdued things. Her fascination with her body had waned, and she didn't want to attract attention via her wardrobe. Instead, she was working on her smile. She wanted to branch out from the Sunday smile and its variations. This was of most concern in terms of her acting. She feared that she was becoming typecast because of the Sunday-School-girl innocence tinted with a cheerleader exuberance. She wanted to have a more haunting, mysterious smile. She certainly felt haunted these days. She went back to the bed and tried to work on the letter to Sam. "I am working on my smile," she wrote. "I want a certain look for future auditions, you see, but at the moment I'm having to retain my All-American wonder for the sake of my dad's campaign. The cameras will be all over me come September." She laughed and tore the letter to shreds. Then her eyes fell on the small Testamaent Cal

had given her when she was a baby. The only way she
knew this was from the inscription inside. Naturally,
she could not remember when he gave it to her. It was
all so weird—the whole thing. Once, she was a tiny dot
in Diana's belly. Then she was traveling down Diana's
dark passageway. Then she was transferred to Mary
Ellen's hands in a dark hall in an ominous brick building near some army base. Then she was in the black-
and-white photos taken in gardens and parishes. And
then she sat forever under the ivory dome of Cal's sanctuary. She felt the old fear and knew it was time to get
absorbed in something other than herself. She picked
up the new script her teacher had given her and imagined herself in all the parts. It worked its usual magic,
and she wrote Sam a long letter describing the kinds of
roles she liked to play.

SEVEN

Sam read the letter on Eva's front porch. It was clear to him that Whitney was in love with drama. In some ways, she reminded him of Diana: She was an actress, and she evaded questions she didn't want to answer. She had not answered his question about their meeting while he was home.

Sam looked down at his legs. He hadn't worked out in almost two weeks. He got up and went inside. He stood by the dresser mirror in his old bedroom. He was blessed with a lot of healthy, dark hair. Most men his age, he knew, were losing theirs. He was considering letting Hazel give him a haircut. Only *considering*, he'd said to Eva. He brushed his hair and examined his face. He was getting brown from Alabama sun. He had that kind of skin. All in all, he decided, he looked all right.

He went into the kitchen and made some instant coffee. Nothing at all had changed in here since he was a boy—same red stool, hotpads, trivets, water jug. He was alone. Eva had gone with Hazel to the doctor—the place over her eyebrow. Aaron had flown back to New York yesterday. He had to be back at work. Sam was to stay on another week, then fly back. He sat at the table and reread Whitney's letter. At the end, she said it had been almost two months since she wrote to Diana in Vermont, that she probably wouldn't write again. Sam wondered what the hell Diana was doing for a living in Vermont. He visualized her on a communal farm, trapped forever in an ideology and lifestyle that certainly bore no fruit nor yielded any degree of happiness. Not that *he* had found any form of utopia living in Manhattan with Aaron, but he was productive. Even if he was static, his work continually evolved and grew, creating a dynamic life of its own, and the life of his work did fuel him with something kin to happiness; or, at least, he knew, when he was in the process of drawing, he felt no pain.

For the third time, he read Whitney's letter. Something began to seep into his understanding of her. A wave of kinship swept him. He looked through Eva's kitchen drawer and found a pencil. He couldn't find paper so he tore the back off the phone directory and began writing. He told her that he knew her fears, though she had not told him what they were; that he was running, too; never to expect to "find" herself through her acting because she was running too hard for that; that self-alienation, which surely she inherited from him (Diana was not serious enough an actress) wasn't a bad thing, that it was part of being an artist, and that her happiest moments would be when she was so far removed from herself that she barely existed. He reread that part. He feared it might be a lie. It didn't matter. He just wanted to know her, he said, because he thought they might be able to be of help to each other. He thanked her for her letter, especially for talking about acting and the kind of roles she liked. He told her he understood that this, too—this talking about acting and roles—was a way she kept her distance from him, but that was O.K. because her letter had ultimately caused him to know some things about her.

He pulled her old letters from his wallet and tried to answer some questions she'd asked about Diana as honestly and in as unprejudiced a way as possible. He told her that Diana's parents were an old Mobile family—a bit of Old South society, that Diana was a renegade debutante, destined to rebel, and that times were ripe in 1966 for her to break like hell from it all. Despite her parents' social life, though, they were "enlightened"—a word Sam disliked but used for lack of something better—and had been involved in the Civil Rights Movement. Diana's father, Charles Zorn, was an attorney and was quite political and influential. He really didn't know much about her mother. Diana had an air of friendliness and was well liked, yet, at the core, she was kind of cold, or at least aloof. She was always up for anything. She liked LSD but she also liked traditional church services. She was zany and a bit spacey—"like most of the people in theater," he added, "and liked to take on gay men." He scratched that part out. He and Diana were friends, he said, close in the sense that they were heavily into "the cause" yet didn't neglect their hedonism for a moment. Sam chose not to describe the night Whitney was conceived—enough honesty for one letter already. What with all the honesty, though, he was tempted to tell her that he, too, was a preacher's kid and if she ever felt crazy, blame it on that. He also wanted to add that he felt sorry for her in this regard

and that he couldn't help but hate her father. Of
course, he left all that unsaid. He ended the letter on a
good note—saying, all in all, Diana had many vibrant
qualities and she, Whitney, had a damn good set of
genes.

The news was bad. Eva felt she should do something
like hold Hazel by the arm—the way she did the
ninety-year-old ladies at the church—as they descended the steps at the outpatient one-day surgery
wing of the hospital. They'd removed the mole, and it
was malignant. Eva knew that melanoma was serious.
Even though bad news was old hat, Eva still felt terribly
sad. It all moved into something more tolerable,
though, on the drive home—a kind of wistfulness.
Hazel had lived next door for over forty years. How
many people in America have the same neighbor that
long? She felt grateful. And Hazel was her old self, for
sure, cracking jokes about the silly shower caps nurses
wore in surgery.

"I told them if there were deadly germs in hair, I'd
have been gone long ago."

"Did you really say that, Hae?"

"Yes, love."

"Want to stop for some lunch? Some hamburgers?"
Eva asked.

"I think not, hon. But if you want some, stop wher-
ever you like, and I'll get coffee."

"I'm not so hungry," Eva said. "But Sam. I thought
I'd get him some Krystal burgers at the drive-thru.
They don't have Krystals in New York. And he loves
them so."

Hazel got an appointment card from the pocket of
her beige pantsuit. "I go back in a week. I guess they'll
whittle away some more."

Eva felt a bit queasy as she ordered the Krystal
burgers, but it passed. When she pulled in to her grav-

eled driveway, she and Hazel parted with a "see you in a while." Eva, clutching the little white sack full of burgers, stopped to look at her garden. It was June fifteenth. The tomatoes, prolific, were still green, the size of plums.

Inside, Sam sat at the kitchen table. All his materials were out. He was drawing.

Eva set the sack on the table, and Sam put his things aside.

"Krystals," she said.

"Thanks." He smiled. Eva watched him get up, walk to the refrigerator, and get the mustard. She knew he would do this. It gave her a good feeling. She believed there was nothing more comforting than your child, grown, in a predictable act—even an insignificant one like getting a jar of mustard.

"They never put enough," he said, holding the jar.

"I know."

Eva sat on the red stool and let her sandals go from her feet. "Hazel has melanoma," she said.

Sam stopped spreading mustard. "That's not good," he said.

"No."

"What did they tell her?"

Eva shrugged. "She didn't say. You know Hazel."

Sam kind of laughed. "You know, I really *don't* know Hazel. Funny you can grow up next to someone and not really know them."

"You were only a child," Eva said.

Sam started spreading the mustard again. "I'm really sorry, Mom. For you, too."

Eva watched Sam eat. She liked to watch Sam eat. That, too, was comforting.

"If you start missing the back of your phone directory, I wrote Whitney a letter on it."

Eva watched Sam take all the pickles off the burgers.

"Well, that's quite all right," she said. "It might be hard to fold, though."

"I'll mail it in one of those big manila envelopes."

"Yes. I'm sure they have them at the five-and-dime."

"Five-and-dime," he said, smiling at the pickles.

"So Aaron tells me her father is running for Congress."

"Right."

"So she'll move to Washington if he wins?"

"I doubt it. She says she's going to the University there in Birmingham for a while. I don't think they can afford to send her anywhere."

"We know about that, don't we?"

"Seems like churches, big ones anyway, like her father probably has, would provide some kind of educational fund, you know?" Sam started eating his third and last burger. "Do we have some Cokes here?"

Eva went to the pantry and got a bottle.

"Oh, this is wonderful," he said, taking it. "A six-ouncer. I didn't think they made these anymore."

"I get them at Ben Ray's." Ben Ray had a gas station —one pump—in town. "You know Sam, Sr., used to say he could tell which ones were bottled up at the plant in Anniston because they used spring water. They tasted better, he said."

"I haven't told Whitney anything about him," Sam said.

"Well, that's understandable."

Eva got up and looked at the pantry shelves. She took down a package of spaghetti, tomato sauce, oregano, and thyme. She picked up the phone and called Hazel. "I'm making spaghetti for supper," she said. Hazel told her to just bring it over, and they'd eat at her place.

"Ask her if she'll cut my hair," Sam said.

Eva asked. Hazel said, naturally, that she would.

At dusk, Eva and Sam went over, toting the pots of spaghetti and sauce. Before supper, they sat on Hazel's front lawn and drank lemonade. She cut Sam's hair there. He was in a straight-back chair, and Hazel's hands worked the scissors, snipping little brown locks that fell into the grass. Eva got one of Hazel's cigarettes —her smoke for the summer. She'd intended to put it off until July, but why not now? Lightning bugs lit up Hazel's yard. A half-moon was directly overhead.

EIGHT

Whitney read Sam's letter. She decided not to show this one to her parents. She knew Mary Ellen would flip over the part about self-alienation not being such a bad thing. The letter was written on part of a phone directory, it appeared, and had arrived in a 9-by-12 envelope. Whitney believed Sam was kind of strange, but she loved him for finally answering her questions about Diana. And the things he'd said about her acting and her running and her fears were painful in their accuracy. It caused her to put the letter at the bottom of a drawer—feeling she would not want to read it again for a couple of years.

She went downstairs. She glanced at her reflection in Mary Ellen's china cabinet. She was wearing an ordinary white shirt and navy-blue skirt, no jewelry, and only a trace of make-up. Her hair was simply combed to the right and tucked behind her ear. Tonight's party was to be in the cafeteria of the steel plant.

Cal and Mary Ellen descended the stairs. They looked dressed for a PTA meeting or a church social. They were holding hands. Whitney pictured them on the cover of a national magazine.

Whitney drove them to the steel plant. Although she'd had her license for quite a while, night driving still bothered her. She kept her eyes glued to the road, and pressed the pedals gently to avoid abrupt stops and starts. Cal sat in the front with her, Mary Ellen in the back. Mary Ellen leaned forward. "I think it's wonderful to have this at the steel plant," she said to Cal. "Don't you?"

"Perfect," he agreed.

"Nat is something else, isn't he?"

"God sent him to us," Cal said.

"I don't know how Nat would take that," Mary Ellen said.

Cal turned to her. "How's that?"

Whitney felt Mary Ellen move up closer to the front seat. "I just don't know if he views the world in that way."

"Oh, I think so," Cal said.

"You think he's spiritual."

"Don't you?" Cal asked her.

"I think he's, above all else, a pragmatist."

"Yes, but I believe he must have a set of beliefs. Why else would he be involved in the campaign?"

"He's a political person," Mary Ellen said.

"But he's got to have reasons for being involved."

"And does it have to be a spiritual agenda?" she asked.

Cal turned back and faced the road. "What do you think, sweetie?" he asked Whitney. She knew she didn't have to answer. She knew he sometimes deferred to her when he was actually just taking time out to contemplate something.

"He comes from a political family," Mary Ellen reminded Cal.

"Which district did his grandfather represent?" Cal asked her.

"Whichever one encompasses greater Huntsville. His name was Nathaniel Hollins, too. Nat was named after him. You know, don't you, that his father is Murray Hollins."

"I didn't know until one of the schoolteachers told me."

"Do you know what year he was appointed to the District Court?" Mary Ellen asked him.

"Seventy-six, I believe."

"Which schoolteacher told you that about Nat's father?" Whitney asked Cal, keeping her eyes glued to the dark highway.

"What, sweetie?"

"Which schoolteacher told you about Nat's dad?"

"I think it was the one who wears the whistle. Why?"

"She knows everything about everybody. She told me Nat should have gone to law school or something like his dad and his granddad, but he made a conscious decision to be a blue-collar worker."

"Oh, I love that," Mary Ellen said.

Cal chuckled. "I believe it," he said. "He seems that way."

"What way?" Whitney asked him.

"Oh, you know, determined to be a common man."

"Like us," Mary Ellen said.

Cal turned back to her. "What do you mean?"

"You know what I mean."

"But we are, aren't we? It doesn't take determination or effort, does it?"

"Cal," she said.

"What?"

"We want to identify with ordinary people, but we aren't ordinary."

"Yes, we are."

"Ordinary people don't run for office. We just identify with and represent ordinary people. Our party does, anyway. Right?"

"I still say we are ordinary," Cal reiterated. "Like Nat."

"The only difference between us and Nat is that he's rebelling against something. That's the way I see it, anyway. But that's O.K. I think that rebellion provides him with a lot of his energy."

Cal turned back to Mary Ellen. "The schoolteacher," he began, then nodded to Whitney, "the one with the whistle. Isn't her name Jena? She told me that Nat hasn't missed a single hour at work."

"He's on seven to three," Mary Ellen said. "He told me he goes in sometimes at five a.m., then takes off at one. That's why he's always there at headquarters in the afternoon. He must not have much of a social life if he goes to bed early enough to be able to be at work the next morning at five. Does he date anyone, Whitney?"

Whitney looked at Mary Ellen in the rearview mirror. "Am I social chairman or something?"

"I just thought you might know. I thought maybe Nat confided in you."

Whitney smiled. "No, Mom."

Whitney had seen the steel plant all her life—from the car whenever they passed it on the highway—but she had never actually been near it. A security guard greeted them at the gate. Whitney rolled down her window, and the man stuck his head in so that he and Whitney were eye to eye. He was old. His face looked like elephant hide, and the smell of liquor filled the car.

"The candidate's family," he yelled. Whitney leaned back.

The man leaned across the front seat and shook Cal's hand.

"I'm Fred," the man said. "Party's in that second building on the left."

Whitney smiled, thanked him, and drove into the parking lot. The room was filled with people. Some were standing, and some sat in chairs that lined the walls. Red, white, and blue crepe paper hung from point to point across the ceiling and along the tables that were set up randomly in the room. People immediately swarmed Cal and Mary Ellen until they disappeared in a sea of bodies. Whitney dodged it all and vanished into anonymity. She spotted a table with hors d'oeuvres. Then she walked around the back wall, looking at the framed photographs of men working in the plant. They wore hard hats, hard expressions, and safety glasses. Some were welding, others drove big cranes, some were bent over furnaces.

"Most of them are unemployed now," Nat's voice said. She turned to face him.

Whitney held her plate out. "Want one?" she asked. "The stuffed mushrooms are great."

Nat took a sausage ball and some almonds. His face looked smudgy, but she knew he'd bathed. She knew every detail of his appearance was calculated precisely. He wore a nice chocolate-colored shirt that set off his dark eyes, and he wore the predictable jeans.

"Ready to work?" he asked her.

"I thought this was a party."

"That's right, it is, but it's a working party. This is a campaign of time donors, not money donors. Understand?"

Nat led her to a table in the far left corner. "Actually, the people with money just keep a low profile," he muttered. An assortment of people sat at the long table. Most Whitney recognized from headquarters but there were some new faces, too. Nat pulled out a chair for her, then he was gone in a flash. One of the women showed her how to fold the paper perfectly so it fit exactly into the envelope. Whitney folded it and passed it to the next person, who put it in the envelope, who passed it along for sealing, who passed it for final stamping. Whitney saw, after a while, that Nat was gradually recruiting more and more people until eventually there were three long tables of workers. Around nine o'clock, a band began setting up—a group of black musicians. A banner near the makeshift stage read Jazz Heritage Band. When they finally began playing, the workers got up and began mingling. Some people danced. Nat sat down by Whitney and put his arm around her.

"How did it go the other night," he asked her.

"When?"

"At your house. How did I do about the Hispanics? The Sanctuary thing?"

Whitney shrugged, smiled, and looked away.

"Ah, come on," he said, gently squeezing her shoulder. "I value your opinion."

"You do?"

"Let's go outside for a while," he said. "It's getting kind of warm in here."

Nat led her out the back of the building. "This is the way I come in every day," he said, "for lunch."

"I forgot you have a job," she said. "I mean, a job other than the campaign."

They sat on a concrete ledge behind the cafeteria building. Straight ahead was a tall fence and, behind it, was a long, low-lying, metallic-looking building. "That's the main plant," Nat said. "Almost every man in Birmingham worked here when I was growing up. The year I was born, this place employed almost 30,000 people. There were coal mines then, ore mines, a nail mill, wire mill, tin mill."

"I've never been here before," Whitney said. "But, of course, I've seen it from the highway. I remember, when I was little, all that fire that used to shoot up in the sky."

"Who knows what's going to happen," Nat said. "The industry is in trouble. Before they built the pipe mill this year, there were only a handful of us still at work."

Whitney stared ahead at the plant.

"I like the school-girl effect," Nat said, gesturing to her white shirt and navy skirt. "Very campaign-like."

"I'm such a natural," Whitney said.

"You remind me of a cat."

"A cat?"

"Slinking. Highly selective about who you brush up against."

Whitney smiled. She liked that.

"Do you have boyfriends?"

Sam had asked her that same question during their first phone conversation. "Sure," she said, "when there's time. I probably won't go out much this summer. I'm taking a beginning theater course at the University, and I'm helping Francy with the Food Bank, and I plan to stay at headquarters a lot."

"That's good news," Nat said. "You're a great campaigner. You work hard."

"It makes me happy to work hard."

"Go America! We need to put you on TV saying, 'It makes me happy to work hard.'"

"Really, it does."

"I believe you." Nat's brow glistened with beads of sweat. It was a typical summer night—hot with a breeze so light you had to see it in moving leaves to make sure you were feeling it.

"You know, you are so different from Cal and Mary Ellen."

"In what ways?"

"They wear their hearts on their sleeves."

Whitney laughed. "Where do I wear mine?"

"I'm not sure. Sometimes I don't feel like I know you very well."

"I don't feel like I know me very well, either." She looked at her hands. "I've been in touch with my birth father." She said it before her usual caution light stopped her.

Nat raised his eyebrows.

"He lives in New York. He's a cartoonist."

"A cartoonist."

"I'll show you some of his things. I know you've heard of the magazines."

"Sure. I'd like to see them."

"His mother lives down in south Alabama, below Selma. He's visiting with her now. He says he wants to get together."

"Well?"

Whitney looked at her hands again. "I'm not sure. Time's running out, though. He'll be leaving in a week. Back to New York."

"What do Cal and Mary Ellen say?"

"You know them. Whatever would make me happy." Whitney got up from the ledge and faced Nat.

"Well, anyway, I'll keep you posted," she said and smiled her Sunday smile, the softer version she'd given Mita and Carlos at headquarters. In fact, she muted it to the point of wondering whether it even formed itself into a smile at all. She glanced up at Nat. Their eyes met, wavered, disengaged. She wiped some sweat off the back of her neck and pulled her hair up for a moment in an effort to cool off. Then she looked at her sandals and Nat's tennis shoes. The sidewalk was dotted with mashed chewing gum, worn into the concrete. Again, she looked at Nat's brown eyes. They had stars of light. They were like magnets. Blues-y music came from the steel plant cafeteria. She stood perfectly still in the heat.

NINE

Nat had worked his first campaign when he was sixteen. He spent that summer in Hattiesburg with his uncle who was running for the Mississippi state senate. Nat's job was as his uncle's chauffeur. He never sat idly in the car though, waiting for the designated affair to conclude. He was there on site—under the giant shade trees at barbecues, in the back of Rotary Club luncheons, even at the old ladies' tea parties—observing.

Since then, there had been a lot of campaigns. Cal's was the first he'd officially managed—and certainly the most important. State senate races and even city mayoral ones were, to Nat, kind of boring and predictable. He knew from the moment Cal announced that he would make inroads early and try eventually to manage the campaign. The district was ripe for change, he felt. The incumbent, Naylor, had served only one term after defeating his predecessor, who had been the district's representative for sixteen years and who, according to Naylor supporters, had grown far too liberal for District 6. Naylor won, Nat knew, because of the incredible organizational strategies of the religious right, who hauled busloads of churchgoing supporters to the polls. The district was caught offguard, and, immediately after Naylor's election, there was alarm over what had happened. Cal was the perfect candidate to defeat him.

Cal intrigued Nat. His urban ministry was appealing, though it presented problems. Cal was handsome. He had an almost eerie presence, Nat thought—an ethereal aura so that, on first meeting, when he took your hand into his big, warm ones and looked *through* you with those unfathomable blue eyes, you felt like you were meeting God. He was gentle yet looked strong. He was very tall. But despite his charisma, there was something potentially self-destructive about him as a candidate, and this was a constant source of disturbance for Nat, mainly because he couldn't put his finger on it exactly. It had something to do with Cal's magnanimity. He was, in essence, as the cliché went, too principled to be in politics. Mary Ellen was another story. Not that she was unprincipled or shrewd or in any way lacked loftiness in her ideals or actions. It was just that she was, in some way, more earthly, rooted in reality.

Whitney was an oddball. He had all kinds of illusions —which he always discarded—as to how she could be used in the campaign. She had a provocative face, perfect for cameras. But Whitney wasn't going to give herself to the campaign in a public way. The thing about her face was that it gave two impressions—a magical dual role. For those who chose to see her from a traditional, innocent viewpoint, she was the quintessential American Girl—blond, blue eyes, natural, and unadorned. But for those who wanted to or were compelled to use their other set of eyes, she appealed painfully to the prurient interest. It had something to do with an elusive imperfection—the slightly crooked front tooth, the wispy blond cowlick on her crown, the delicate birthmark below her ear. Nat had looked at her in the former manner until the night of the party at the steel plant. It was at the precise moment when she wiped the sweat from her neck and held her hair up that he'd seen what he assumed others must see. The value of this remarkable duality, in terms of the campaign, was that, either way, people would find her pleasing and would want to make sure they saw her again.

Francy arrived at his apartment building at nine-thirty on Sunday morning. To make what he considered a Cal-like magnanimous gesture of reconciliation after the fight he'd had with her over the Hispanics, he'd agreed to go to church. He'd never heard Cal preach, and he knew this was neglectful on his part in terms of knowing his candidate from every angle. His fear of entering churches, though, had kept him from doing his job thoroughly. Very few things blocked him from doing his job thoroughly. Francy blew the horn. He was trying to tie his tie. He went onto the balcony. "Come on in, for Chrissake," he yelled.

Francy appeared at his door a few seconds later. "That's a nice Sunday salutation, Nat," she said. He looked her over. She looked like a recovering anorexic church secretary dressed for church. She wore a big ivory dress, plenty roomy to conceal her skin-and-bones body, and carried a tiny, ladylike purse in one hand—surely, he imagined, it contained one of Cal's colorful 3-by-5 notepads. He smiled into the mirror over his mantel as he readjusted his tie.

"What is it, boss? Are you happy this morning?"

"Not in the least."

"You're smiling."

"I was thinking you probably have one of Cal's little notebooks in your purse."

Francy opened it. "Wrong," she said. It was empty.

"What are you carrying it for?" he asked, giving up on the tie. He tossed it on the couch where his cat slept and unbuttoned his shirt at the neck.

"To keep my hands occupied during the service," Francy said.

"Are you nervous, too?" he asked her.

"Of course not. I just like to have something in my hands."

Francy scanned the apartment. "Nice place," she said.

It was a wreck. Nat appreciated her courtesy—weren't you supposed to say something like that the first time you visited somebody's home?

"Thanks," he said, "but, really, Francy, it's not a nice place, is it?"

"Well," she said, "you need a maid, Nat."

"A *maid?*"

"Yes. I know a lot of single guys who have maids." Francy walked over to the secretary that had belonged to his great-aunt. "Nat, this is lovely," she said. "I love antiques."

"Is that one?" He knew it was, but he was embarrassed by its presence.

Francy surveyed the dining room. "And that table!" she exclaimed.

He felt his neck redden. "It was my great-grandmother's," he said. "It would have hurt my mother's feelings if I hadn't accepted it."

"Why are you apologizing?" she asked him. She ran her hands over the wood.

"Do you mind if I look around?" she asked him, eyeing the bedroom door.

"No," he said. "Go ahead."

He brushed cat hairs from his dark pants and looked at himself once more in the mirror over the mantel. He knew Francy would have something to say about the quilt on his bed.

"Nat," she called.

"My mother made it," he said.

Francy appeared back at the door that led to the bedroom. "You really have some fine things here," she said and looked at him with scrutiny. "You like nice things, don't you?"

Yes, he liked nice things but it wasn't something he liked to think about or talk about. This, his place, was private, and he never had his buddies over. They met for lunch or beer (though he didn't drink because he didn't like to get sluggish) after work or for parties sometimes, but it was never here at his apartment. He didn't want to hear the banter about the antiques, the quilts, and the china (his grandmother's, which he kept, discreetly, in a china cabinet on the back porch). Women didn't come here, either. He took them out, to other places, and if he knew the night was going to end in bed, he made sure it was at the woman's place and not his. If you let somebody see where you live, see your things, then you're exposed.

He considered trying to explain this to Francy. She was standing in the doorway, smiling at him knowingly, like she understood all of it, anyway, so he figured there was really nothing he needed to say.

"You're something, boss," she said.

"I am?"

"Yes."

He looked at himself a final time in the mirror. "Do I look O.K.?"

"You look great."

"O.K. without a tie?"

"Sure."

"But will everybody else have one on?"

She waved it away. "Forget it," she said. She glanced at the door to the kitchen.

"Go ahead," he said. "Make your inspection complete."

"I'm sure your dishes are appropriately dirty and scattered about," she said, "to hide your true, elegant little self."

If this were anyone but Francy, he would be infuriated, but Francy was different. He was beginning to think of her as part of himself, a voice of conscience, a wise old friend. He smiled at her.

They walked down the three flights of stairs. "Do you see anybody on a regular basis?" she asked him.

"Yes," he said. "I see you on a regular basis."

"O.K., boss. But you know what I'm asking."

"I don't see anyone now," he told her.

"And before?"

They rounded the last flight, and stepped out into the incredible morning light. It hurt his eyes.

"I lived with a woman for three years."

"In love?" she pursued.

"Yes."

"Who ended it?" she asked him. "Let me re-phrase. Who started seeing somebody else?"

He looked at her. He considered lying, but Francy was the kind of woman you didn't have to lie to in order to put yourself in a good light. "I did," he said.

"And what happened with the new one?"

"We split up a few months ago."

"Who did the splitting?"

"I did."

"Why?"

He opened the car door for her. "The campaign started."

She looked at him and frowned. "Is that a reason to break up with somebody?"

"Yes."

"O.K., boss. I'll take your word for it," she said and slid into the front seat.

Actually, it just wasn't right from the first—this most recent relationship. She was an attorney, and they were both too busy to get anything going.

On the way, Francy stopped at the twenty-four-hour donut shop on Magnolia Avenue and bought some raspberry-filled donuts. They tasted great. Nat licked his fingers and felt that the sugar rush would at least carry him through the sanctuary entrance.

"These are good," he said. "You're a great date, Francy."

"No problem. I do this every Sunday."

"So what's Cal preaching on today?"

"I didn't pay much attention when I was typing. I was listening to a short-wave radio station, Radio Havana. I'm working on my Spanish. But anyway, the title of the sermon is 'Celebration.'"

Francy parked the car in the church parking lot in a space that had Krueger painted in perfect lettering on the curb. "Hey, this is first-class," he said. "Your own place." Cal's car was next to hers. Next to his was an empty place with Drake painted on the curb. "That's the choir director. Damn him, he's always late. It drives Cal crazy. You'd never know it, of course."

"Right," Nat said.

They walked around to the front entrance. The big fountain was on, spewing water up in arcs. The grass beside it was trashed from the bar-hopping Saturday night crowd that loitered by the fountain on the church lawn till midnight. Nat looked up the street at head-quarters and wished he was there instead of here.

"Please," he whispered to Francy. "The back row."

"That's where the teenagers sit," she said, "but never mind, most are on vacation."

A man handed Nat a program. On the front was a picture of the church. "Calvin Gaines, Pastor," was underneath it. The print was high-quality. Nat had forgotten that there was old Birmingham family money floating around Cal's church. They sat in the back pew. Francy patted his knee. The congregation was a potpourri, all right. There were some older people wearing "money" on their suits and dresses, but there were also Southside street people, some from the neighborhood halfway homes, he knew, from things Francy had told him, others from the shelter places. And, of course, there were the Hispanic faces and a variety of international people that Nat knew took part in the conversational English classes. Shortly, the organist chimed eleven notes, and Nat looked at his watch. Right on the dot. "Here comes Drake," Francy whispered and nodded toward the choir loft. "He's pushing it to the limit." Cal stood up from his massive chair behind the pulpit, smiled, and raised his arms. With that, everyone stood and began singing. Francy opened the hymnal. The song was "This Is My Father's World."

"Watch Mary Ellen," Francy said.

Nat did not sing, but listened while he watched Mary Ellen's hands signing:

This is my father's world,
and to my listening ears,
All nature sings, and round me rings
The music of the spheres.
This is my father's world,
I rest me in the thought
Of rocks and trees, of skies and seas
His hand the wonders wrought.

This is my father's world,
the birds their carols raise;
The morning light, the lily white
Declare their maker's praise.

Mary Ellen smiled whenever she'd sign the "father's world" part. She was wearing a dress the color of morning sky. Nat sighted Whitney over behind the deaf congregation. She stood alone, holding a hymnal. She sang, but Nat knew she was somewhere else. She was gazing over to the stained glass on the left side of the dome-shaped sanctuary. It was a cross between a wistful look and a bored one. Cal knew the words by heart. So, rather than looking at a hymnal, he searched the eyes of his congregation. Nat felt, for the first time, certain that Cal and Mary Ellen and Whitney were incapable of losing.

After the service was over, Francy took Nat and Whitney to lunch. "On me," she told them, reaching into the glove compartment for her wallet, as they pulled out of the church parking lot. They went to a barbecue place on the north side of town—down by the railroad tracks and warehouses. "We won't see anybody we know," Francy said. "Fame is hard to bear."

Whitney smiled and looked out the window. She was in the back seat. Nat was watching her through the mirror attached to the sun visor on his side of the car.

Francy turned on the radio and began searching for a station. "So what did you think, Nathaniel? Were you saved?"

"I was very impressed. They've got quite an act."

Francy gave him a look. He didn't know how to tell her, in Whitney's presence, that he was in love with the whole family. Love wasn't the right word, anyway. He understood that these kinds of strong feelings surfaced during campaigns. The thing about Cal and Mary Ellen's service, though, was that it was hard to think about God when you were so caught up in the two of them. He knew they intended, as Mary Ellen had told

him once, "to reflect the light," but they were light itself. He glanced back at Whitney. She was writing
something in one of Cal's little notebooks—a green
one.

"Are you recording this conversation?" he asked her.

"Hardly," she said.

Francy leaned up so she could see Whitney in her
rear-view mirror. "You're writing a poem," she said,
and they smiled at each other in the mirror. "She hates
poetry," Francy explained to Nat.

"Well," Nat said and turned around to face her.

"Well, what?" Whitney asked.

"What are you writing?"

"I'm drawing a picture of an elephant," she said.

Francy giggled. "That means mind your own business, Nathaniel."

"Do you keep journals?" he pursued.

Whitney put her pen in her lap on top of the paper.
He could see words but not what they said. "No, I
don't," Whitney replied. "Do you?"

"No."

"I never did, either," Francy said, "until I joined the
group. Part of therapy is journal-keeping. It's really a
good thing to do. Mary Ellen keeps one."

"I bet," Nat said.

"I hope you're logging the campaign," Nat said to
Francy. "You could make a lot of money someday when
Cal is president."

He glanced at Whitney in the mirror. She smiled that
vague smile again, out the window.

"I don't record *information*, Nat. I record my *feelings*,"
Francy said.

"Well, forget the fame, then. Nobody gives a shit
about feelings."

Whitney laughed.

"Actually, that's not true," Francy said. "There have
been a lot of books about feelings. Ask Mary Ellen. I
bet she could give you a list of at least ten books, off the

top of her head, with 'feelings' in the title."

"Isn't that just left-over riff-raff from the seventies?"

Francy turned in to the barbecue place parking lot. Smoke rose from the chimney of the old brick establishment. Old Pit was painted on the door.

"You know I did record something about the campaign. I recorded how I felt after our conversation at headquarters that night."

"I'd like to read it."

They went inside.

The booths had seats of dark-red, torn vinyl. The menu had a drawing of a pig on it. The selections were handwritten. Nat and Francy sat across from Whitney. The waitress, a big, pasty-looking woman with a warm smile, slid three glasses of ice water over the tabletop. She took a pad from her apron pocket.

"Ready to order?"

"Sure," Nat said. "I'll have a barbecue plate."

"Salad or slaw?"

"Salad."

"Dressing?"

"Thousand Island."

"French fries or potato salad?"

"Fries."

Whitney ordered a cheeseburger and potato salad, Francy a salad with vinegar.

"Francy," Whitney said.

"What?"

"Is that all?"

"I'll have some iced tea," Francy added.

"Bring her a barbecue sandwich," Nat told the waitress.

The waitress left. Francy laid her wallet on the table, and Nat felt her cross her legs under the table. "You'd think I was somebody from the half-way house," she said, "the way you all run my business."

Francy got up and went to the jukebox. Nat watched her body move in the loose ivory dress. He wondered what kind of things went through someone's mind who was deliberately starving to death.

"She's never been married, right?" he asked Whitney.

"Right."

"Ever been serious about anybody?"

Whitney shrugged. "I don't think so. There was a guy, a long time ago, I was only twelve maybe, and I can't remember much about it. I wasn't paying attention to everybody's love-life in those days."

She smiled her crooked-tooth smile.

"And are you now?" he asked her.

"Yes."

He looked at her hands, folded on the table. The nails were squarish. There was a hint of color.

Francy returned to the booth and slid in.

"The man behind you is wearing a Naylor button," she whispered. "They're talking."

Nat looked at Whitney. Whitney looked back and forth from Nat to Francy. Nobody said anything. The waitress brought their food. Nat poured ketchup all over his fries until they were drenched in red. Francy glanced over. "Steelworker," she said. Then they were all quiet again. Nat listened while he ate. One of the men had a booming voice, the other was barely audible. The boomer said, "A pinko all dressed up in a preacher's robe," then laughed at what he'd said.

"He's got a strong following," the other one said softly.

"Teachers and the like," the boomer said.

"My son's a teacher."

"Yeah. Well, don't blame yourself," the boomer said and laughed. The other one laughed, too.

"Hmm. Good, isn't it. The sauce is the best in town. They got somebody knows what he's doing back in the kitchen."

The waitress passed and apparently stopped at their booth. "No thank you, honey, that'll be all for us. Just the check," the boomer said.

Nat wished like hell he could turn around and see what these guys looked like. His back was to them.

"Can you see them?" he asked Whitney.

She took a bite of her cheeseburger. "The one who's not so loud," she said.

"No person in their right mind could support his platform," the quiet one said.

"All kinds of fools in this town. The country's going to hell in a handbasket."

"Cal Gaines is going to hell."

Nat and Whitney and Francy looked at one another.

T E N

Cal's office window faced west. He wrote in late afternon when the sun fell over his desk in long, gold sheets tinted various shades depending on the season and angle of the sun. Today, he sat with pencil in hand, tiny red notebook open but empty. He always composed in miniature like this—scribbling in his little pads with a No. 2. Nat knew these things from conversations with Francy. And, indeed, he found Cal in just this pose—behind his giant cherry desk, late afternoon sun streaming in and over his hands that cradled the tiny pad and pencil. He wrote furiously like a reporter jotting juicy details, yet Nat knew—from his preaching last Sunday—that whatever Cal was creating was bold and sweeping. "I still have enough fundamentalism left in me to believe the virgin birth," he'd told Nat once. "A God who can make stars can surely impregnate a woman." Nat found this amusing yet noteworthy.

Today, he wasn't sure why he wanted to see Cal. He'd gotten off work at three and gone directly to headquarters where he had called Cal's office. Francy had answered.

"Boss!" she'd said. "What can I do for you?"

"I need to make an appointment with the big boss," he'd told her.

"He's very busy," she said with obvious affectation.

"I'm sure."

"Come on over, fool. You don't need an appointment."

He left headquarters and crossed the street to the side where Cal's church stood. He stopped at the hot-dog stand and ordered five chili dogs and a bag of chips. Inside the church basement, he got a Coke from the machine, walked through the big room that had Fellowship Hall over the door, and headed for the elevator. He stopped. By the TV set in matching lounge chairs sat two women—clearly the most identical of all identical twins he'd ever seen. They looked young—early twenties, were attractive, and wore red ruffly dresses.

"Hi there," one of them said. "You here for the meeting?"

"No. I'm on my way up to see Cal."

He was eating one of the chili dogs. Suddenly, he wished he'd gone home to change clothes. He was back in production now, spending most of the shift operating the new q-bop furnaces. He needed a shower.

"O.K." she said and smiled. "I thought you might be here early for the meeting. It's at five."

"No," he said and swallowed the bite of chili dog. He smiled and got on the elevator.

Francy's desk was behind a long glass window on the main hall of what they called the "education building," adjacent to the sanctuary. He smiled at her through the glass then opened the door.

"Hey," she said and looked at him over her half-rimmed glasses. She was wearing long, dangling earrings. Nat went over to her and touched them. "What are these?" he asked.

"Seagulls."

He examined them. They were, indeed, gold seagulls.

"Listen, I just saw a set of identical twins in the basement. They were watching TV."

"Yes," Francy said. "And?"

"That's all. I just thought it was strange. They looked just alike."

"Most twins do."

"O.K., Ms. Krueger. Here," he said and gave her a chili dog. Francy looked at it like it was a dangerous object.

"They are here for the A.A. meeting," Francy said. "Those twins are. They co-lead the group."

"They're *both* drunks?" Nat asked.

"Recovering alcoholics."

"Well, I'll be damned."

Francy continued to stare at the chili dog. "It's from Dino's," Nat said. "It doesn't have onions."

"It is too hot to eat chili. It's July."

Nat opened the hotdog wrapper and scraped the chili off with a sheet of typing paper onto another sheet of typing paper then wadded both pieces up and threw them into a trash can. "Now," he said.

"You know," Francy said, taking off her glasses and her seagull earrings, placing them on her desk, then folding her hands, "you are actually more obsessed with food than I am. You remind me of my mother."

Then she picked up her phone and buzzed Cal's com-line. "There's an unsaved steelworker here to see you."

"I love you," Nat said.

"I'm sure you do."

Francy opened Cal's door for Nat, smiled, and gave him a tender hug. She was really a good woman. He liked her a lot. Nat found Cal in his predictable pose—at his desk, the stream of light, the tiny notepad.

Nat handed Cal a chili dog.

"Thank you," Cal said. "I could use one." Nat ate the other two, and they shared the bag of chips and Coke.

"Glad the voters can't see this office," Nat said, between bites. "It would ruin things."

The rug was plush, an aqua color. The furniture was nice wood—cherry, he believed—and there were some fine machines, too—a word processor, audiovisual equipment, a fancy telephone system.

"You must have some tithing doctors in your congregation," Nat said and gave his hotdog wrappers to Cal, who threw them into a trashcan under his desk.

"Yes, we do. As a matter of fact, we are having a special commissioning service for three of them next Sunday. They're leaving for El Salvador to help set up a new clinic there."

"Well, that's great," Nat said. This kind of politically volatile information drove him crazy.

"We'd like to see you in church again this Sunday," Cal added.

"You're sounding more like a preacher every day," Nat said.

Cal smiled.

Nat wiped his face and hands with a handkerchief and leaned forward. "Seriously, Cal, it was a terrific service. You are a born orator."

Cal leaned back in his plush chair, running his big hands along the arms of it. Nat wanted to retract or at least modify the last statement. He was beginning to feel, in Cal's presence, the same way he felt in Whit-

ney's and Mary Ellen's for that matter—that he was raw
and secular and spiritually unrefined.

"Of course, I know it's more than oratorical excellence that you seek or have found."

Cal looked at him with the impenetrable blue eyes.
"Yes, that's true. I've lived what I preach."

Nat wanted to pursue that, but didn't.

"On the other hand," Cal continued and turned his
attention to the window, the street below, "this may surprise you, but, in seminary, we are videotaped as we
deliver our first sermons so we can watch ourselves and
'polish our act' so to speak. What do you think Jesus
would think of that?"

"I haven't the slightest idea," Nat said and meant it.

"It disturbed me then. It still does."

"I bet you looked great, though, on tape."

"Yes. And I loved it." Cal turned back to Nat. "That's
what disturbs me. And that ties in with the campaign,
you see. It takes a lot, I mean a lot, of self-absorption to
run for office—to relish crowds and cameras and controversy. I would like to think I'm doing this as a noble,
altruistic pursuit. It's not that way. It can't be, can it?"

Nat didn't know. He didn't say anything.

"The love of the pulpit can become a dangerous entity. That's why," Cal leaned over toward Nat, "it's important to work hard on days other than Sunday—the
Food Bank, our Hispanic friends, all that out there."
And he pointed out the window. Cal leaned closer and
smiled. They were eyeball-to-eyeball. "I guess I needed
to talk, didn't I? Did God send you here?"

"I don't know," Nat said. "I was sitting up at headquarters, thinking how good a Dino's chili dog would
taste, and the church was right next to Dino's, and I
thought you might want one, too. Does God work
through hotdogs?"

"Of course," Cal said. Nat believed he was serious.
He looked at his boots against the aqua rug, recalling

he did have a reason for coming. He just wasn't sure what it was.

"After church Sunday, Francy took us to the Old Pit for lunch."

"Good barbecue," Cal said.

"Yeah, it was great."

Nat looked at Cal's tie. It was blue with gold designs —triangles or something. "Did Whitney tell you about the conversation we overheard?"

"No." Cal got up and adjusted the venetian blinds so that the room took on a muted, amber light. Nat hadn't intended to stay this long.

"So tell me," Cal said, "about the conversation."

"It was Naylor's people—just the usual trash, you know, nothing noteworthy. It's just that I was worried about Whitney."

Cal looked pained.

Nat continued, "But if she didn't mention it to you, probably she was all right."

Cal picked up a paper clip and turned it over and over, tapping it lightly on his desk. "That's not necessarily true. Whitney keeps most everything to herself, especially things that she believes might upset people."

A family trait, Nat thought, but didn't say. He wanted to talk about Whitney—*that's* why he was here, but it wasn't, he knew, strictly out of concern for her well-being. He just wanted to talk about her.

"You know, I didn't really discuss this candidacy as much as I should have with her, prior to announcing. I guess this is a common source of guilt for anybody who runs—the effect on children."

"Whitney's very adaptable," Nat said, "don't you think?"

"I should have talked to her more."

"Why did you decide to run?" Nat asked him.

Cal tapped the paper clip against his desk again. "I love this city," Cal told him.

Nat nodded.

"I hated to see it so misrepresented. You know, Naylor's last campaign was organized by outsiders."

"Texas," Nat said.

Cal glanced up. "Texas?"

"Texas."

Cal smiled. "I guess you know more about all that than I do."

Nat nodded. He knew just about everything there was to know about how local campaigns were funded and plotted.

"It makes sense," Cal affirmed. "Most of the fundamentalism in our conference comes from out that way."

"What's the thing that gets you the most?"

"About Naylor?"

"Yeah."

"Censorship."

Nat nodded.

"All books have value," Cal said.

Nat looked at Cal's desk top.

"I would not have ever run," Cal said, "if I hadn't been encouraged so strongly by the community."

"Who?" Nat asked with keen curiosity.

"City Council members. Church members, of course." Cal leaned forward. "But, I can tell you the night I knew it was inevitable—it was when the mayor came over. I will never forget our conversation. We talked about Birmingham. We talked history. Injustice. Justice. Progress. Dreams. We cried."

Nat felt a vague sense of indignation. Like, there were things that had transpired between Cal and other significant people that didn't involve Nat. It was almost unthinkable that the campaign had a life of its own before he—Nat—became a part of it.

"It all made sense, then," Cal said. "So much sense that I just didn't cover all my bases at home." Cal looked at his big hands. "I mean with Whitney. The self-absorption thing I was talking about. You can get so self-absorbed, so certain that you have this *mission,* that you forget your children." Cal shook his head and put the paper clip aside.

"Whitney likes campaigning," Nat noted.

Cal didn't respond. He was staring at the window, even though the venetian blinds blocked the view of anything. Nat glanced around—the ivory walls, aqua rug, bookcase full of spiritual titles. It was a soothing place. He imagined people coming here for solace and to have great questions answered.

"Well, I'll be moving on," Nat said finally. "Need to get back to headquarters then on home for a shower and dinner."

"No," Cal said. "Don't go yet, O.K.?"

Nat sat still.

Cal moved in closer again. "What did the Naylor people say at the Old Pit?"

Nat hesitated.

"They said you were going to hell."

Cal threw his head back and laughed heartily. It was the first time Nat had heard him laugh. Always the smile, but never a laugh. It was heartening.

"Come on over for dinner," Cal said.

Nat looked at his watch. "I need to go home really. Need a shower, to feed the cat."

"Fine. Come at seven."

At the Old Pit, Whitney had felt it rising inside like heat. The feeling was vaguely recognizable, though distinctively new. It reminded her of early fear—the first time she saw lightning in a storm, or first sexual desire —that kind of sweeping sensation. She didn't know what to call it. She only knew, at the moment, that the words "Cal Gaines is going to hell" were causing a physical reaction in her. Days later, sitting on her front porch at dusk, she knew it was called rage. The word had come to her, inexplicably, while watching workmen over in the Hardys' yard—gathering materials up from the day's work. The Hardys were getting a new roof. The men had bare, bronze backs that glistened with sweat. Whitney was looking at them through the screen that was flecked with residual spring pollen—it had been unbearably heavy this year. The July heat was unbearable, too. And, for some reason, the sun on those laborers' naked backs had given her the word "rage." It was a relief finding a label for the feeling. That way, she could can it, label it, and store it—just the way Mary Ellen did blackberry jam. Whitney liked to operate this way. Her mother's idea of "exploring your feelings" was crazy.

When Nat arrived for dinner, he was wearing his beige slacks and a shirt that looked suspiciously Central American. It was worn casually (not tucked in) and had a mixture of orange and blues cast into a floral design. When she greeted him on the porch, she noted the shirt and asked him if he was joining the Sanctuary Movement.

"Right," he'd said.

"Well, you do look like you've just returned from Guatemala."

Nat looked down at his clothes. Whitney believed that his cheeks had reddened. She'd never known him to be embarrassed over anything.

"I thought you might be up to something," she baited, smiling, trying to lighten things up again. "You know, like you and Francy had another argument, and you're here on some mission to bend Mom and Dad's thinking." She tilted her head and gave him a variation of the Sunday smile—the one used to put people at ease.

Nat sat on the porch ledge. The last of the sun fell on his face. He kept looking at her funny. It made her uncomfortable.

"What have you been doing?" he asked her.

"In general?"

"Well, today."

"I've been sitting here thinking about rage."

"Thinking about rage," he repeated.

"Yes."

"*Thinking* about it or feeling it?"

"Just thinking."

"Oh." Nat shook his head and looked at her again in that funny way. She felt like he was studying her.

"I felt rage at the Old Pit," Whitney said. "That's all."

"And when you think about it, about those men *now*, you don't feel the rage again?"

"No. Just the memory of it."

"That must be nice," he said, "to get over something so quick. I mean, I'm the kind of person, as you probably know, who can't, ah, who holds grudges. I can still muster up some rage when I remember things that happened to me twenty years ago."

"Ugh. That's awful."

"Well, if you want another dose of rage, you can read tonight's paper," he said. He held it, rolled up, in his hand. He gave her a swat on the knee with it, and went inside. Whitney sat there, on the porch, for another twenty minutes or so, not wanting to see the newspaper or Cal or Mary Ellen or Nat or whatever lay ahead anywhere past the next few minutes of solitude on the front porch. This was getting to be familiar—this not wanting to move forward another inch for fear of new discoveries that might force her to feel things.

Now, though, she made herself get up and go inside. The kitchen table looked incredibly small—the way her parents and Nat were all huddled over the newspaper, pointing to things and talking softly. Whitney slid into the empty chair and looked at her mother. Mary Ellen smiled that painful smile—like her face might break at any moment.

"What's going on?" Whitney asked, nodding toward the newspaper.

She looked down. There was a big picture of Cal's

church and, next to it, one of Cal taken in his office. He was at his desk, leaning back in typical pastoral pose. It was under the section of the paper marked "Religion." Whitney knew this section ran weekly on Friday nights. Her parents always read the section because it contained news of local churches.

"I had no idea," Cal said to Nat. "If I had, of course I would have talked it over with you. Well, naturally, I wouldn't have agreed to it in the first place."

Whitney looked again to Mary Ellen for information. Mary Ellen took her hand and said. "It's the weekly interview, you know, that they always do with a minister in town. The 'what's-going-on-in-your-church?' thing. We believe that the man who interviewed Dad must be opposed to his candidacy. The article brings too much attention to our Hispanic families."

"Well, it's worse than that," Cal said. "I sound like a lawbreaker." He smiled weakly. "I guess we are, aren't we?"

"So was Martin Luther King," Mary Ellen said.

"This city didn't think much of him, either," Cal noted. "Can you imagine District 6 electing him to Congress?"

"Things have changed," Mary Ellen said.

"Look, guys," Nat said. "It's probably not going to amount to much. If it was in any other part of the paper, I'd worry. But this Religion section is so obscure and boring, I doubt if the article will be read."

"Obscure and boring," Cal said and gave Nat a look.

"Right. Don't take it personally, reverend. Be grateful, in this case, that you chose such a bland profession."

"I wish that were true. It's too colorful for words," Mary Ellen said glibly. She turned to Whitney. "Isn't it, sweetie?"

Whitney kind of smiled and didn't say anything. The only excitement she knew about was when a deacon walked up to the altar and punched Cal out for saying that the church doors were open to all God's children, meaning blacks. And that was before she was born. It was a story Cal told at parties.

"I'm just sorry," Cal said to Nat. "I should have talked it over with you first."

"You don't owe me any apologies," Nat said. "You're the boss."

"That remains a point of confusion for me," Cal said.

"Well, anyway, it's all done with now. Forget it."

"Let's eat," Mary Ellen said. She got up from the table and took the sizzling roast from the oven.

ELEVEN

"This is her father, her adoptive one," Eva told Hazel. Eva liked the way he looked in his big desk chair—handsome and pensive.

"Looks like a big deal he's got there," Hazel said, pointing to the photograph of Cal's church beside the one of him. Whitney had mailed the newspaper article to Sam. It arrived the day before he left to return to New York, and he'd given it to Eva.

Eva looked at Cal's face. "My granddaughter's father," she mused. "What does that make us—me and him—in terms of kin? I'm a strange bird, Hae. I have a son and a son-in-law. I have a granddaughter who's got parents I've never met."

"You're doing better than me, love. I don't have a soul on earth."

It was true. Hazel's husband died back in 1960 with black lung. There were no children and not even a niece or nephew. Hazel had more friends than anyone Eva knew, though.

They sat at Eva's kitchen table. It was covered with ripe, red tomatoes Eva had gathered from the garden. She was canning today. Mid-morning sun flooded the room.

"Sam left me something else," Eva said. She went over to the drawer underneath her cabinets and opened it. The picture of herself that Whitney had first sent to Sam lay on top of the matchbox. Eva got it and took it over to Hazel.

"Oh, what a doll!' Hazel said. "Look at that hair—the color of wheat and so healthy. I bet no one ever gave this child a permanent. Aren't you proud of her, love?"

Eva took the picture from Hazel. "She has Sam's teeth. See that front one? Just a tad crooked."

"It's cute. I'm glad they didn't put her in braces, aren't you?"

Eva studied Whitney's face from all angles.

"I bet you can't believe she's yours." Hazel said.

"She's not," Eva said.

"Sure she is, love."

"Well, maybe she'll come down to visit sometime." Eva put the picture in her apron pocket and dropped some more tomatoes into the boiling water over the stove to loosen the skin for peeling. She glanced up at the clock. At noon, they were leaving for the hospital. Hazel was being admitted for a couple of days to finish all the tests—scanning the organs to see if the melanoma had spread. *A clean bill of health.* Those words kept coming to mind—spoken to Eva many times by the fortunate—friends who had survived heart attacks and subsequent bypass surgery, acquaintances who had strokes that left only a trace of sluggishness in the right arm or the left leg, and women with benign breast knots. She imagined it—Hazel phoning from her hospital room, "A clean bill of health, love."

The old station wagon was hot, but once they got on the highway to Selma—past the traffic lights—the wide-open road allowed the breeze to circulate. And the humidity had succumbed a bit to the high pressure system that had moved in the night before. Eva's hair blew away from her face. It felt good. They were in the very heart of summer—a miserable place to be—yet she was all right. Knowing you're in the eye of the storm, that it won't get any worse—this, Eva knew, provided her with iron strength. She'd felt this, most acutely, twice in her life—during the height of each labor pain birthing Sam, and at the moment she discovered Sam, Sr., wired up to his bed. She knew she had a natural capacity to endure, a kind of emotional endorphin overflow, she supposed, recalling the flood of strength she'd experienced at horrible moments.

They arrived at the hospital right at one. Eva carried one of Hazel's suitcases, and Hazel toted the other. Eva scanned the gift shop while Hazel admitted herself—searching for postcards for Aaron. She found one with big trees draped with Spanish moss. She scribbled a note on it: "Aaron, this is what things look like down here now. Hot. Sultry. Tomatoes are in. Canned this A.M. At hospital with Hae. Will call. Love, E." She bought a stamp and dropped the card in the hospital mail chute in the lobby.

Hazel stood by the elevator.

"O.K., love. Room 312. Let's go."

They rode up. Hazel's room was bright, fresh, and sunlit. It was already full of florist vases filled with assortments of daisies, carnations, and roses—sent with well-wishes from friends who knew she was going in today for tests.

"You're a popular woman," Eva said.

"It's a sweet thing, isn't it, love?"

Eva read the names on the cards. Most were Hazel's "ladies" along with a church member or two.

Hazel sat on the edge of the bed. "Well, what am I supposed to do now? Put on a nightgown and look sick?"

"Yes. And buzz for a pain pill," Eva added.

"Right. And adjust and readjust my bed."

"Right. And complain about it."

Eva sat in the chair.

"Are you worried?" she asked Hazel.

Hazel, still sitting on the edge of the bed, stared out the window. "What's there to worry about?"

Eva smiled, didn't pursue it further. She knew what Hazel meant. If the news was bad, it was just one more thing in life to pass through. She understood with clarity that she and Hazel shared a philosophy of life— even though she couldn't define it. They were troopers, comrades in a war against something she couldn't name.

Eva sat in her parlor in the loveseat underneath the painting of a girl playing a harp. It was another bright, blue-sky day—and she was waiting for the flood of strength to encompass her. Hazel had called that morning, and her bill of health wasn't a clean one. The melanoma had spread to the lymph system, and there was a spot on her lung. Eva had absorbed the information. It was one of those *bad moments*, she knew, and she needed the exhilarating to blend itself with the excruciating. Instead, she was feeling a very simple, but paralyzing, sadness. She got up and went to her garden. The vegetables had already passed their peak, though, and the foliage was beginning to fade and turn brown at the edges. Finding no solace there, she went back inside and called Sam. She listened to the distant New York ring, and then Sam's voice.

"It's Mom," she said.

"We were just talking about you," he said.

"It must have been a most pleasant conversation."

"It was," he laughed.

"And how are things? How's Aaron?"

"He's making an Indian dish for supper. The apartment smells like curry."

"Hmm. I don't use curry often."

"So how are things? What's going on there?"

"Sam, Hazel's tests were bad. It's spread."

"Where?"

"Lymph system and lung."

"The liver will go next."

Eva didn't say anything.

"We had a friend," he reminded her. "That's how hers went anyway. I'm sorry. I'm really sorry."

"They're going to try an experimental drug, Hazel says."

"That's not treatment, that's research. Just a minute. Let me fill Aaron in."

Eva heard him telling Aaron, in so many words, that Hazel was dying. He returned to the phone, and Eva moved on to other things. How was his flight back? She'd enjoyed having him home. He mentioned the Krystal burgers and Whitney's last letter. And would she check the newsstand in Selma, whenever she was up that way, for the Birmingham paper—he was curious about Cal's candidacy.

"Just a second, Mom. Aaron wants to talk to you."

She waited.

"Hello, Eva."

"Hi, honey. What're you seasoning with, besides curry?"

"Oh, some red pepper, garlic. Listen, Eva, I'm so sorry about Hazel. I know you must be feeling low."

"Yes," she said, and she felt kind of choked. Aaron's tender ways. "I'm sad."

"Of course you are. Eva, I want you to do something, O.K."

Eva waited.

"I want you to go through your cedar chest and begin collecting things—heirlooms, keepsakes, whatever—for Whitney."

Eva didn't say anything. Why should she do that?

"I've been thinking about this, and now's a good time to start doing it, don't you think?"

"Well, I don't know."

"Don't know what?"

"I don't know when I'd ever see her or what I'd tell her or why she would want these old things in the first place. It's mostly junk."

"The cameo, Eva, that was your mother's, the one you showed me, that's not junk."

"The one for my daughter-in-law."

"Right."

They both laughed. They had a running joke about the things Eva had planned to give to her daughter-in-law someday. The cameo, especially, had provided them a laugh, early on, in the first year or so of Sam and Aaron's relationship, when Eva was still adjusting and needed some humor to ease it all. "It just doesn't go with my suit, Eva," Aaron had told her.

Now, Aaron was reminding her. "You've got a granddaughter, Eva. That's a hell of a lot better than a daughter-in-law. She's your own flesh and blood."

"Yes, that's true."

Eva glanced out the window.. The sight of Hazel's jalousie-windowed porch almost pulled her back under, but she stayed above water. Yes, it was a good idea that Aaron had.

"O.K., honey," she said. "I'll open the cedar chest as soon as we hang up the phone."

"O.K. Sam's in the kitchen messing up my cooking. I

need to go. Call us again later in the week."

She hung up. She made herself a cup of camomile tea and thought long and hard about a cigarette. She even got out an ashtray—the one shaped like a scallop shell—and placed it in front of her. But she'd already had her summer smoke, she wasn't due one until fall, and anyway Hazel wasn't home to provide the cheating cigarette. Still, she had a key to Hazel's place. She knew there was a cabinet full of Pall Mall cartons in the shop. *No.* She sat awhile longer and basked in her iron will. This was more like it—a knight in heavy armor. All was perfectly quiet—her place, the neighborhood, hot summer dusk.

Finally, she got up and moved to her bedroom. It was the westernmost spot in her home. The sun had already set, but a salmon-colored afterglow lingered, causing the dusty place to look oddly sprinkled with face powder. She stood by her vanity and looked at herself in all three parts of the mirror. She was wearing a Sunday dress—a floral print in shades of violet. She never wore a dress on weekdays, but the trip to the hospital had necessitated it today. Her skin was the color of ginger, attributable to long days in the garden along with her Cherokee Indian heritage. The dark skin against the violet dress was pleasing, she knew. She might pass for a chic widow just home from a trip to the Caribbean, if it weren't for the dingy fingers and calloused knees. "Well," she said aloud, undressed, and slipped into the familiar, comforting brown shorts and top. The first thing she did was to get some masking tape from the drawer and a pen. She tore off a piece, stuck it to the back of the vanity, and wrote *"Whitney"* on it. She did the same on her cedar chest, chest-of-drawers, and roll-top desk. This was the poor man's rite of bestowal, the unwritten will—these little pieces of tape on the back of furniture. When her mother had died, the daughters went through her belongings, checking the backs or underneaths of tables, chairs,

beds, and vanities to find their legacies. Eva's name—
she was the oldest—was on the back of all the pieces of
her mother's bedroom suite. She knew they were pur-
chased for a small mite years ago by her mother, but by
the time they reached Whitney's hands, they'd be valu-
able antiques. She opened her cedar chest and got the
jewelry box containing the cameo, a delicate opal ring,
and some old coins. There was no need to mark these
because she knew already that she would give them to
her long before she died—along with the double-wed-
ding-ring-design quilt on her bed. Eva went to her parlor and studied the china cabinet. She taped it, wrote
"*Aaron*" on it, and then realized there was nothing for
Sam. She pulled the tape up and wrote Sam's name
instead. The piano! Yes, of course, the piano would be
Aaron's. But how on earth would they transport the
china cabinet and piano to New York? Well, it wasn't
her problem, and, anyway, she somehow felt that, by
then, Sam would have come to his senses and moved
back home. This new wave of generativity was exhilarating. She was not alone. She had a son, a son-in-law,
and a granddaughter—hardly a basic, ideal family,
but it was *hers*. She sat at the piano and played "Stars
Fell on Alabama" over and over until her rusty handling of the keyboard oiled itself into a fluid and lyri-
cal repose.

Sam stared at the wall. It was bare. That's how he
liked it, or, more precisely, that's how it had to be in
order for him to work. He did not tolerate distractions
well. He began inking over the pencil sketching he'd
done last night on the vellum paper, erasing, adding,
maximizing the composition of each panel, until he was
happy enough with it to put it over the lightboard and
begin the final tracing onto the Bristol board. Whitney
had sent the article about her father, but that was all—
no letter, no response to his heart-pouring. It left him

feeling disarmed and almost panicked. To deal with this, he was doing a satirical series on the religious left. He knew it was, in a way, a betrayal to Whitney, but you did what you had to do. His only regret was that he had left the article back in Alabama with his mother. He'd like to have it on hand to refresh his memory, get him in the mood, and also to have some basic information to help him with the strips. Also, he wanted to see Cal's face. It caused a storm of feelings that fueled him with energy to draw. It was hard to imagine how Cal's life had mapped itself. Was his father a minister, too? God, was everybody's? No. Aaron's wasn't. He was a butcher. Sam heard something sizzling in the kitchen. The Indian dish was probably almost done. He was running out of time for the evening. He never drew after dinner. Generally, he and Aaron sat for an hour or so at the table and talked—lately about Whitney, Cal, Alabama politics, and why it was not feasible to consider moving.

Predictably, right at seven, Aaron's voice called, "It's ready."

Sam lay his Rapidograph and crowquill pens aside, by the Bristol board, and went to the kitchen table. There was a big dish of rice and some colorful food in the skillet—which Aaron had set on a trivet Eva had given him. "Looks great," Sam said. He picked up a cube of meat and studied it. It was a ruddy color. There were specks of green in the sauce.

"Don't play in it," Aaron scolded. "Eat it."

Sam looked at the meat.

"Stop acting like it's alive," Aaron added.

Sam took a bite. "Great," he said as he chewed. "Really great."

They ate mostly in silence, not due to any ill-feeling, just because they always did it that way. Even in the early days, meals were a serious matter. Talk was for afterwards, over coffee.

Sam cleared the table, put on the coffee, and

spooned a scoop of Häagen Dazs into silver dishes for both of them. A faint breeze came in from the open window. Still, it was hot. Sam unbuttoned his shirt. "Do you want coffee?" he asked Aaron.

"No. Forget it. Too hot."

Sam cut off the coffee-maker, and they ate the ice cream and drank water. Aaron leaned forward, elbows on the Formica-top dinette table.

"What're you working on?"

"The religious left."

"I might have guessed."

"They're an easy mark."

"What if it sells? What if they see it?"

"They?"

"Whitney and her parents."

"Don't worry. People don't read magazines in Alabama."

"They don't?"

"No," Sam said. His spoon clinked against the cold metal dish as he got the last dregs of his ice cream.

"That's a sweeping statement."

Sam went to the refrigerator and looked for something else to eat. He got the fresh strawberries that Aaron had washed and put in a Tupperware container.

"How do you know nobody reads magazines in Alabama?" Aaron asked, jostling the ice in his water glass. "You haven't lived there in over twenty years."

"You sound like a Confederate, defending your homeland," Sam said. He offered Aaron a strawberry.

"It might be a good place to live now."

Sam knew that Aaron was going to make a pitch, now, to move to Alabama.

"You like isolation rooms?"

Aaron looked at him. "I've never been in one," he said. "Have you?"

"Yes. I grew up in one."

"I bet it's different now."

"You bet *what's* different?" Sam pursued.

"The people are."

"So what if they are?" Sam said. "That doesn't change the fact that you'd never see another play or show or movie for the rest of your life."

"We never go anyway." Aaron reminded him.

Sam considered this. It didn't seem like it was true, but he was having a hard time remembering the last time they saw anything.

"Anyway, doesn't Selma have theaters?" Aaron persisted.

Sam shook his head and laughed. "You just don't have any idea what it's like."

"The next time I talk to Eva, I'm going to ask her to look at the paper and tell me what's playing in Selma," Aaron said.

"You do that."

They looked at each other. Sam hoped Aaron was getting irritated. He loved watching him fight anger. There was something oddly arousing about it.

"So," Aaron said. "Is that the only problem? Dramatics?"

Sam looked at him. He was so incredibly blind to things Sam felt were clear as day. "Friends?" Sam asked him. "Have you considered like-minded people?"

"We don't see anybody anymore. You know that."

"But they're there," Sam said. "And we do see them."

Sam knew he was right about this one. True, the network was smaller since they'd settled in than it was a few years ago, but it was more intimate in ways, and they certainly had some good friends. He began recounting silently the number of times they'd had people over for dinner during the past year and the times they'd been treated to the same.

Aaron shrugged. "We'd have them down to visit. We'd meet people there, too, don't you think?"

Sam reached over and shook Aaron's shoulder as if trying to jar some sense into him. "There's nobody like us there. Can't you understand that?"

"Not a single gay man in the state of Alabama?" Aaron asked flatly.

"If there were, we'd never know it," Sam said. "People don't acknowledge things there."

Aaron looked intensely into Sam's eyes. "How do you know that?" he said. "You haven't lived there in twenty years."

"I really wish you'd stop saying that."

"It's true!"

Aaron picked up the hotpad he'd used to bring the skillet to the table. It was shaped like a turkey. He turned it over from side to side, reflectively staring at the table. "Eva is going to have a hard time with Hazel's illness."

Sam got up, put the strawberries in the refrigerator, and opened the freezer door, letting the frigid vapors swirl into his face. The kitchen was unthinkably hot.

"What're you doing?" Aaron asked him.

"I'm standing here thinking it's this hot six months out of the year back home."

"I like to be hot."

Sam smiled and tousled Aaron's blond curls as he moved to sit back down at the table.

Aaron looked at him, boyishly. "You know, Eva will need you nearby when Hazel goes."

"You want to move into Hazel's house, right, when she dies, get your cosmetology license, and look at ladies' gray heads all day. No, you want to bring in the Boys Ranch outside Selma, *charity work* mind you, and clip young heads."

"Sounds great," Aaron said. "Listen, I'm telling you, I'm not going to live the next ten years in this apartment. I don't want to grow old with you in Manhattan."

"You want to grow old in Pineapple, Alabama?"

"Well, not necessarily, but where else would we go? Ames, Iowa? Amarillo, Texas? Waycross, Georgia? I mean, it does make sense, doesn't it? Isn't this what people do? Don't they move back home? Don't they take care of their living parents?"

"Your parents don't live in Pineapple."

"If you think I'm moving upstate," Aaron interrupted, "you're crazy. Anyway, my dad won't be alive in another couple years. What's wrong with you? I don't get it. You can live anywhere. You aren't tied to a job here. You never do a damn thing anyway but sit behind that desk and draw. You could do that anywhere. Why not do it somewhere nice? Where it's pretty. Where everybody's O.K. Where we can *kick back* for God's sake."

Sam savored this. He really liked Aaron mad. It was so unusual that, when it did happen, it took on an exotic flavor—all that blood rushing to his boyish face, hands gesturing madly like an actor getting into a character totally foreign to himself.

Sam gave him an exaggerated look of love.

"Stop it," Aaron snapped.

Sam sat back, in mock fear.

The heat of Aaron's anger was dropping rapidly now—evident in his face—to a boring state of sulking. Sam quickly switched gears. "I understand," he said. "And I agree."

"With what?"

"With everything you said."

"And, so, what? What does that mean?" Aaron stood up.

"It means I agree with you."

"A kind of inactive agreement?" Aaron asked.

"What's that?"

"I mean, you agree that we *should* leave this place, but you don't necessarily agree that we *will*," Aaron concluded.

Sam looked at his own hands, still brown from being in Eva's yard for two weeks. It was honestly the first time in his life he'd considered going home—on a permanent basis—and it was all tied up with Whitney. It all depended.

"It all depends," he said to Aaron.

Aaron sat back down. "On what?"

On the outcome of the election, he wanted to say, but he couldn't say it. He didn't know how honest he could be with Aaron or with himself. He'd always operated on the notion that if you say something out loud to somebody, to anybody, it becomes fact. If you just mull it over silently, it's still not necessarily true. Best not to think aloud. For this reason, he was a private person and had, for most of his life, been accused of being a ruminator. Despite the criticism this invited and the obvious barrier to intimacy with Aaron—the first person he'd even come close to trusting—it was the only way to live. His last letter to Whitney had clearly violated this, his own safety code, and he regretted deeply this effusive error. Anyway, he'd definitely thought it all out—this dreadful move back home, back to the closed minds and small worlds. So, what if Cal lost the election, didn't move to Washington, and Whitney stayed there with her family and went to the University and maybe even wanted to have a relationship with him, and Aaron got to have his little farmhouse in the backwoods, and Eva lived happily ever after with her boys nearby, and all that? Did he hold the cards to everybody's happiness but his own? No, Whitney held them. No, Cal did. No, the people of Birmingham did, the small-minded, right-wing, hard-ass voters of the 6th Congressional District of Alabama did. Oh, God, what an unspeakable fact.

TWELVE

Cal's father wasn't a minister. He was a sportscaster. He called the Birmingham Barons' baseball game at Rickwood Field on the city's northside in the forties and fifties. Cal knew, from conversations overheard and just child's intuition, that his father was a womanizer. He knew, from just plain old eyesight, that he was a heavy boozer—but a high-spirited, good-natured man who stayed in the early stages of alcoholism for a remarkably long time, long enough for Cal to grow up and get into seminary, out of his father's world, before the bad part began. He had died ten years ago. Most of Cal's memories were of the dusty baseball diamond, eating sno-cones underneath the bleachers, staring up at the undersides of human beings while his father's voice blared over the loudspeaker—that's how he told it all to Nat anyway. They were at headquarters. It was August first. It was dark. Cal was in a mood that Nat liked. There was an edge to his voice, it lacked the pastoral self-assuredness. He was just this *man* who'd grown up with a zany, drunk father who hauled him to baseball games he didn't like, leaving him—the shy kid —to hide in the dirt under the bleachers.

"Maybe that's why you became a preacher," Nat said.

"Why's that?"

"Staring up at people's asses all the time. You know, it must have given you a certain view of life, like there was work to do in the world, a bad side to people."

Cal laughed—heartily—just as he'd done in his office that day. Either he was changing or Nat was just getting to know him better. They were in the usual metal folding chairs at headquarters, leaning over the old wooden desk, looking out the long window at the bar people roaming the streets—most of them kind of stylish and having fun. Headquarters was empty, except for Nat and Cal.

"It's like we should have been raised by each other's fathers," Nat commented.

Cal looked at him quizzically.

"I mean, my father is this quiet, conservative, well-mannered lawyer/judge, and I come up a steelworker who can't sit still. And you have this wild, crazy man for a father, and you come up a preacher."

"Who can sit still?"

"Well, long enough to write a sermon. Hell, long enough to write a book. I've never seen one of your books."

Cal looked at him. "They're not thrillers."

"I can imagine."

They sat in silence for a minute or so. "I could use something to eat," Cal said. "You?"

"Sure."

"Dino's?" Cal asked.

Nat reached for his wallet, but Cal stopped him. "No way. I owe you, remember?" Cal took out his wallet and opened it. Nat saw a picture of Whitney—probably made at school—and he had a fleeting desire to grab it, so he might study it and figure out exactly what it was that kept pulling at him.

"Hotdog? Fries? What?" Cal asked.

"A couple of hotdogs. A Coke."

"Be back in a minute," Cal said.

Nat watched him go out the door and pass by the window. He had the build of a retired basketball player. Nat was beginning to feel bad about this thing, whatever it was, with Whitney. I mean, this was Cal's daughter. Not that he felt sexual about her, just that the sight of her hurt. He was, he figured, fifteen years older than Whitney and ten years younger than Cal. But, however innocent all his thoughts concerning Whitney, her age, his age, his place in the Gaines family might be, it did cause enough guilt to make him jump when the headquarters phone rang just then.

It was Francy.

"Nat. Listen. This is just awful. Is Cal there?"

Nat stood up, phone in hand. "What?"

"It's about Rosa."

Nat sat back down, relieved, and a bit mad at Francy for scaring the hell out of him.

"What?" he said.

"Is Cal there?"

"No, he's at Dino's."

"It's just awful."

"Well, what is it? Is she sick? Is she dead?" He hated to be so blunt, but it drove him crazy for people to not get to the point.

"Well, she probably will be, Nat. She sure as hell

probably will be," Francy said, the pace of her words building in anger.

"What's going on, Francy? Just tell me what you're talking about."

"She's being deported."

"How do you know?"

"She *told* me. The INS people were at the Lintons' house today. She called me while they were there. The Lintons are out of town, on vacation, at the Gulf or somewhere, and the INS people were there. Mita and Carlos, too, of course—they're all being deported. It was the articles, Nat. I'm telling you, those Naylor people may think they're just waging a campaign, but they're not, they're causing people to go home to death squads."

"Well, they have family there, don't they, in El Salvador? Won't they keep them safe?"

"Oh, Nat, you're so damn dumb. When's Cal coming back?"

"Well, as long as it takes to walk to Dino's, get hotdogs, and walk back up here. You know the distance. What do you want me to do? Have him call you?"

Her voice softened. "No, just talk to me until he gets back, O.K.? I didn't mean to call you dumb. I'm just in knots, that's all."

"Nothing new, huh."

"Right, Nat."

"Things are quiet here," he said.

"Have you gone over the schedule yet with Cal?"

"No."

"I talked to the schoolteachers yesterday afternoon. They're going to get the yard signs Monday. That zoo fellow, what's his name?"

"Yarbrough."

"Yeah. He'll have the posters ready by next week. Did you know he lives at the zoo? He's got a house there. He built it. It has concrete floors, and the heating comes up through pipes. In winter, you take off your shoes when you go in so that the heat can reach you. It comes through your feet."

"That's something."

"He has children. Can you imagine growing up at the zoo? Think about his daughters—I think he has girls. Think what it would be like to have a boy pick you up for a date at the zoo."

"It would be something," Nat said.

"He's a good artist, though," Francy said. "He's directed the zoo for twenty years. Can you believe that? You know what he looks like, don't you?"

"Yeah."

"Does he look a day over thirty to you?"

"It's hard to say."

"Somebody, well, I'll tell you who it was, it was Coley, the archeologist told me that Yarbrough, the zoo guy, has a nudist colony in north Alabama. I think he founded it even. Do you believe that?"

"Francy, are you anxious?"

"You didn't answer my question. Do you think there's a nudist colony in north Alabama?"

"Francy, you're chatty."

"I'm what?"

"Chatty."

"I'm sorry," she said sadly. "Yes, I'm anxious. Is Cal back? Go look out the window."

Nat got up, stretching the phone cord. He saw Cal lumbering up the street with the little bag of hotdogs.

"He's coming," Nat said. "Look, Francy, try not to worry, O.K.?"

"O.K., boss."

"I love you."

"I know. I love you, too."

"Just hold on a minute."

Nat put the phone down and met Cal at the door.

"Francy's on the phone," Nat said. "She's upset. Don't worry, it's not your family. It's about Rosa."

Cal put the sack down on the desk.

"Francy," he said into the phone.

Nat went to the back, to the storeroom, and sat in the dentist's chair. He didn't want to listen to Cal's side of this conversation. He hated to see all this unfold. The first article, the one in the Religion section a month ago, had been kind of bad, but nothing compared to the ones that had been appearing since then. It was all part of the campaign coverage, but it seemed that somebody was all too willing to give Naylor an opportunity to talk about Cal and the Sanctuary Movement. But this—this deportation business—was more than he'd ever imagined: the Immigration and Naturalization Service making its way to Birmingham to deport Rosa and her cousins. It was ludicrous.

"It's ludicrous," he told Cal later.

They were sitting in the storeroom. Nat had gotten up and offered Cal the dentist's chair, which he had accepted readily—as if it were a psychiatrist's couch he knew he was obligated to take at this point. Nat leaned up against the shelves stacked with the attorney's stationery and envelopes.

"Yes," Cal agreed. "It is ludicrous."

"You believe it was the articles?"

"Of course it was," Cal said. "It—our involvement—is not something we hide, you see. But, on the other hand, it's not something we display in the newspaper."

"I understand," Nat said.

"But, then, we generally don't run for office," Cal said. Then he looked out into the hall, his face suddenly so ashen that Nat turned quickly to see what horrible thing Cal was seeing.

There was nothing in the hall, nothing visible. Nat believed, though, that he understood what it was that Cal was beginning to see.

"I have sinned," Cal said.

"You've sinned?"

"Yes."

"Is it a sin to run for office?"

"When you put people's lives in jeopardy to fulfill your own selfish needs, you have sinned. Don't you think?"

Cal looked at him earnestly as if he, Nat, could answer a theological question.

"I don't know," Nat said. "I don't know anything about that way of thinking."

"That must be nice," Cal said. He said it dreamily, with wistful fascination. "To live that way must be nice."

Nat shrugged.

"You probably carry other kinds of burdens, though."

Nat looked at him. "Like what?"

"Alienation."

"From what?"

"I don't know," Cal said. "I'm not you."

Nat looked at him. It wasn't like Cal to use this kind of circular reasoning. He did not want to see Cal fall apart in this dentist's chair.

"Listen, why don't we go to your house?" Nat said. "If that's O.K. with you. I mean, if you don't mind me coming along."

Cal smiled at him gratefully. "That's good. That's right. That's the right thing to do."

"I'll lock up," Nat said. "You go on, and I'll be right behind you."

When Cal was out the door and in his car, Nat picked up the phone and called Mary Ellen. Francy had already called her with the news about Rosa. Mary Ellen sounded very normal—a big relief.

"He's upset," Nat said. "You know, kind of weird."

"You mean depressed?"

"Well, yeah. I guess that *is* what you'd call it. I didn't mean that word 'weird' in a bad way."

"I understand perfectly," Mary Ellen said. "Cal does appear weird when he's depressed."

Nat hung up, feeling like Mary Ellen was the only solid person in the campaign, including himself.

"Don't let him drop out," Nat said, very pointedly, to Whitney. She was on the screened front porch when he arrived, and Mary Ellen had told her the whole deal apparently—the thing about Rosa and also that her father was depressed."

"Don't worry," she said. "He'll get over it."

"He's really down."

Whitney brushed some lint or something off her dress. She was wearing a peasant-looking thing that hung to her ankles, and she was barefoot.

"It's kind of a critical juncture, you know," Nat continued.

Whitney didn't say anything.

"I mean in the campaign."

Whitney looked at him vacantly.

"You know, I feel like most of my conversations with you are one-way."

Whitney smiled at him in a peculiar way.

"You can understand why I feel that way, can't you?"

"Sure," Whitney said. "You do most of the talking. That's O.K., isn't it?" Her peculiar smile broadened to a charming one.

"So did Mary Ellen tell you everything?" he asked her.

"Rosa's already on the plane. So are her cousins."

"That quick?"

"That's what Mom said."

"Are you upset over it?"

Whitney got up from her rocker. Nat was sitting on the banister so that Whitney was now taller, standing over him. Her sapphire eyes carried a demure look. "Of course it's a bad thing, but we absorb a lot of bad news in this house—every time somebody dies, or al-

most dies, or wants to die, or is gonna die." She gently
tucked her hair behind her ear, drawing Nat's attention
to the birthmark underneath it. "A lot of news travels
in and out of here. Most of it's bad." She kept standing
over him. He tried to avoid looking at her lips.

"That dress you've got on," he said. "It reminds me
of something from 1969."

"I was three in 1969," she said. "What about it does?
You mean because it's long and drab and ordinary?"

"Yeah, that, also all this stuff," he said, pointing to
the way it laced up the front like a shoe.

"I wore it in a play," she said.

"Oh," he said. "That explains it."

"Explains what?"

"It just doesn't look like something you'd buy."

"It was Mom's."

"You're kidding."

"No."

"I can't imagine Mary Ellen wearing something like
that."

"Well, she was alive, you know, in 1969. She didn't go
to another planet during all that."

"Yeah. I've just never thought about it—what it was
like for them."

Whitney shrugged. "Don't ask me."

They heard a car door slam. Nat turned. It was
Francy. She came up the steps to the porch. "Hi," she
said. She hugged Whitney intensely and shut her eyes
tight—like there *had* been news of a death. Nat
watched Whitney's face. She had the vacant expression,
but she did pat Francy's back gently—in a kind of ob-
ligatory fashion. They all went inside. Cal and Mary
Ellen sat in the den. The Central American motif made
Nat uneasy for reasons he didn't fully understand—it
was all so bright and busy, and Cal was still ashen.
There was more embracing, and Nat felt like the guy at
the funeral home who really didn't know the deceased
too well, who's witnessing grief at a distance.

Cal was on the sofa, holding on to a decorative turquoise pillow, kind of patting it like it was a small animal. He was losing it, all right. Mary Ellen sat next to him, leaning forward, bronze hands tightly clasped on top of tightly pressed bronze knees, her gorgeous face restricted by its necessary role, Nat concluded, *wife of depressed minister.* She struck him as the kind of woman who might dance on tables if given the right situation —only she understood all too well that the die was cast the other way, that life had dealt her a hand that demanded temperance and modesty. And she handled this all with exquisite grace. It's just that her face always looked on the verge of breaking into something other than what it was forced to hold—imminent laughter or tears or seduction.

"Coffee?" she asked Nat.

"Yes. Great."

"Juice?" she asked everybody else. They all shook their heads, no.

Mary Ellen left the room. Nat heard the noise of the beans being ground. He hoped there wouldn't be any tears over the fact that it was Guatemalan coffee.

Francy and Nat sat in the matching rattan chairs. Whitney was in the recliner. She looked incredibly relaxed, legs propped, ankles crossed. The dress continued to fascinate Nat. It was the color of wet sand.

"Has anybody called the Lintons?" Cal asked Francy.

"We don't know how to reach them. They're staying at somebody's condominium in Destin, but nobody knows whose it is."

Cal put the turquoise pillow aside. Nat was glad to see this. It was disturbing to watch him pet it. "Well," Cal said.

Francy tilted her head, waiting for him to go on.

"I guess we need to notify the other families."

"I've already done that. The Turners and the Baldwins say that nobody's knocked on their doors. The Freemans weren't home."

"Doesn't it stand to reason, though, that they—the INS—would know of the others. Apparently, they've been investigating us."

"I just don't understand," Nat interrupted, "why here? Birmingham. Aren't we—I mean, you, you all, your church—aren't you the only group in the city who's doing this? Why don't they pick on those places where they come in? Like New Mexico, Arizona, Texas?"

Mary Ellen returned with Nat's coffee. "They do," she said to him. "They already have."

"Rosa and Mita and Carlos are just drops in the bucket," Francy said to Nat. "There have been thousands of deportations, you know."

Nat didn't know. He didn't know anything.

"This isn't the first time we've been through this," Mary Ellen said to him.

Nat found this information heartening. Soon, things would be back to normal.

"It is the first time we've been responsible, though," Cal said.

"We lost a Guatemalan girl a few years ago," Mary Ellen explained.

"I didn't feel responsible for what happened then," Cal reiterated. He looked at Nat. "There's only one thing to do," he said.

Nat knew this was coming.

"Drop out," Cal said.

Nobody said anything.

Nat glanced over to Whitney. Her frightened face unnerved him. It was the first time he'd seen that look on her.

Nat got up and walked all over the den. Then he went to the kitchen. He picked up a dish towel. There was a recipe in Spanish printed on it. There was no way to escape the Hispanic slant to this household. No wonder Whitney was strange—growing up with foreigners and death lurking in every corner.

"O.K.," he said, stepping back down into the sunken den. He stood by Francy's chair and directed his words to Cal. "What you need to do is to let us take over. Let Francy handle the INS—if they're still around here. I'd love to watch Francy go at it with the INS, wouldn't you?"

Cal didn't respond, but a smile lit Mary Ellen's face.

Nat knelt by Francy's chair, to get face-to-face with her. "O.K.?"

"Right, boss," she said gingerly.

Yeah. How had they all lived without him all these years?

To Cal, he said, "Let me handle the news people—if they know—and forget the campaign. The school-teachers are doing the yard signs. The posters will be ready next week. You just (go somewhere and pray, he wanted to say)—you just lay low, take it easy, and forget the campaign. It's August. Don't forget that. It was a hundred and two degrees today, did you know that? Never make a decision in Alabama in August."

"I think he's right, Cal," Francy said.

Mary Ellen went to the kitchen and returned with a plate of teacakes. "One of the better things about the ministry," she said to Nat, offering him one. "People are always baking you something."

"It's hardly worth it, is it?" Francy asked Mary Ellen.

The two women smiled at one another and lightly touched hands.

Nat ran his fingers through his hair.

"I need to go," he said. He looked at his watch.

"A date?" Francy asked him.

"Yes."

He and Cal exchanged good words, that they'd talk tomorrow, and Nat walked toward the living room.

It wasn't until he was reaching for the brass front-doorknob that he realized Whitney was right behind him. He turned, faced her. "Thanks," she said. Her lean arms hung to her sides, their length accentuated by the droopy peasant dress. Her waif smile faded right as she grabbed him, then she immediately let go and vanished, back to her family's sunken den. It was a split-second embrace, like an insect bite—over before he knew what had stung him.

Whitney sat on her mother's cedar chest. Mary Ellen was unmaking the bed. She folded the bright yellow spread back and fluffed up the feather pillows. Cal was still in the den, but he was reading one of his Spanish newspapers, and Whitney knew this meant he was doing O.K. since it was something he did for pleasure —it gave him a good feeling to know he could translate so easily.

"So Dad's staying in the race, you think?"

Mary Ellen gave her pillow one last toss and sat on the edge of the queen-size bed. "I don't know, sweetie. How do you feel about this?"

Whitney smiled—another *feelings* question.

"O.K., what do you *think* about it?"

"I don't want him to quit."

Mary Ellen nodded. Active listening.

"I think he can win."

Mary Ellen nodded.

"I mean, what would happen to the yard signs and the new posters, and all these people? Wouldn't they be disappointed?"

"They've worked in other campaigns, and there will be more after this one."

"But isn't this one kind of special?"

"Well, of course it is, to us."

Whitney looked into the Guatemalan designs on Mary Ellen's bathrobe and asked her the question that had been needling her all night. "Is this what happened to Maria? Was she deported, too?"

"Yes."

"That's awful."

Mary Ellen signed something Whitney didn't understand. It almost looked like she was making the sign of the cross, which was real strange since they were Protestant.

"What was that?"

"Just talking to myself," Mary Ellen said, and they laughed. Then, more seriously, Mary Ellen added, "It was a prayer."

Whitney looked at her hands, then at Mary Ellen's. Their nails were painted the same color, but it was more than the polish that gave her the feeling they were hands from the same mold. They were almost identical in structure—the squarish nails, the prominent knuckles, the way the pointer finger turned inward slightly. Yet, their hands were not related, genetically. Her mother had an adoption poem that began, "I did not plant you, true." It was about discovering a seedling that somebody else has planted and nurturing it until it bears fruit. Whitney genuinely wished she had a greater tolerance for poetry.

She told Mary Ellen goodnight, went up to her room, and sat cross-legged on the rust-colored spread. The church had provided a daybed for Maria when she was here. Some deacons had moved it to the Gaineses' house, up the stairs, and into Whitney's room. It was still there, pushed against the other wall. Whitney looked at all the accumulated junk she'd stashed on it —wadded up sheets of paper, cassette tapes, childhood teddy bears, and maps. A map of Birmingham, a map of Alabama, the United States, Washington, Central America, and a few topos that covered places like the Sipsey Wilderness in north Alabama and Oak Mountain State Park—places where she'd camped with friends she met in her orienteering class last summer. A new map was second only to a new script in terms of solitary pleasure.

It was hard to believe Maria had slept here—night after night—and Whitney didn't even ask her one single question. I was only fifteen that year, she argued with this new part of herself—this godawful conscience. Still, it was bad. Maria was back in Guatemala or El Salvador or whichever one it was, and, from what she gathered, it wasn't cool at all to leave and then come back. They, whoever the bad guys were, let you know it, too. She was beginning to feel real bad. Time to think of something else. What? Maria's daybed kept drawing her attention. She considered writing to her. But, what was there to say? Sorry I didn't ask you any questions. Sorry you're there instead of here in my bedroom. Ugh, was this the way life was going to be? Regrets? What was she doing, right now, or not doing, that would give her this bad feeling on down the road? Sam. O.K. She was going to do something about Sam.

She got a piece of paper and a pen. It was going to be succinct. "Dear Sam, I want to get together. Bring Aaron along. I know you are afraid to explain about you and him, but don't worry, I already know." She tore it up and started over. "Dear Sam, I'd like to invite you (and Aaron, if you'd like) to come to Birmingham in the fall. I'm sure Mom and Dad would be delighted." She tore that up, too. She got up, went to her drawer, and got the three articles that had appeared in the paper about Cal and Sanctuary. She got an envelope and stuffed them in. She scribbled a note. "Sam, why don't you come to Birmingham in November after the election is over. Love, Whitney."

T H I R T E E N

She was more like Diana than Sam wanted to believe. This deliberate (or so it seemed) enigmatic posturing.

"Maybe she's just shy." Aaron suggested.

They were having a late breakfast. It was Saturday morning. Whitney's scribbly note along with Cal's articles had arrived in the morning mail. Sam sat at the table in his bathrobe, eating blueberry yogurt, scanning the articles.

"So, that's Cal," Aaron commented, leaning over, studying the photo that appeared above his quote. "It is our Judeo-Christian heritage. The idea of sanctuary begins in the Book of Exodus."

"Why do you think she keeps sending me these things?"

"Maybe she just wants you to know what's going on." Aaron, still hovering, got up under Sam's face. "That's not a complaint, I hope. I mean, you're certainly exploiting it to the fullest."

Sam had completed the piece on political preachers. He liked it. It was clear Aaron didn't.

Aaron took some biscuits from the oven and set them on the table.

"Well, do you think he's attractive?"

Sam tossed the articles aside and left the table. It wasn't a question he wanted to consider, much less answer aloud. Of course he was attractive, and Aaron knew it. But, again, if he kept it to himself, if he didn't acknowledge that he thought so, aloud, then it remained not necessarily true.

He sat down at his desk and looked at the comforting blank wall in front of him.

"I'm sorry," Aaron said.

He hated for Aaron to apologize when he hadn't done anything. It was a reminder that Aaron was a better person than he was.

"These biscuits are good," Aaron said. "And getting cold."

Sam got up. It hurt Aaron's feelings when he didn't eat.

He sat down at the table again and buttered a biscuit. Then he poured honey on it and some of the blueberry yogurt still left in the carton. Aaron smiled.

"Drown it," he said.

Sam liked to pour things on food. It was one southern thing about himself he just couldn't shed. He used ketchup on nearly everything.

"Are you mad at me?" Aaron asked him.

"Of course not."

"So, back to what you were saying, how is Whitney like Diana?"

"Hell, I don't know. It's pure conjecture. I only know her through these notes she scribbles, and I haven't seen Diana in eighteen years. Do you think she's serious about this getting together in November?"

"She said so, didn't she?" Aaron asked.

"Yeah, but maybe she just feels sorry for me or something."

Sam knew this kind of self-degrading statement was out of character, and wasn't surprised at Aaron's laugh. "You sound like a sixteen-year-old pining over his dream-girl."

"That's about it."

"Does this orange juice taste funny to you?" Aaron asked.

Sam took a sip. "No," he said. "It tastes all right. You know, I believe Diana enjoyed being pregnant, this role of martyred young woman, carrying her unwanted child, doing her time at the Christian home for unwed mothers."

"Why didn't she get an abortion?"

"I'm telling you, you just couldn't get one. Not in Alabama in 1966, not a safe one anyway."

"But couldn't she have gone somewhere else? To another state? Georgia even, couldn't she have gone to Atlanta maybe?"

Sam shrugged. "Maybe so, But, that's what I mean, I think she wanted to carry this thing to its fullest dramatic conclusion."

"You didn't like her very much, did you?"

Sam drank up his juice and poured another glass. "She was all right." He stared at the glass in front of him. "She wasn't a very warm person." Sam looked at Aaron. "I don't guess I am either, though."

"Was she pretty?"

"She had these incredible eyes. Very blue and translucent, like big marbles. As best I recall, she didn't have to use eye makeup on stage, they were so startling. Is that possible?"

"Are you sure it was you? Are you sure you were the father?"

"Is any man?"

"Well, I take it things were pretty crazy."

"Yeah. To be honest, I can't believe the kid is normal."

"Why?" Aaron smiled. "Were you tripping?"

"Oh, sure, that was a given. But there were other things going on, too."

"Like?"

Sam waved it away. He wasn't sure he remembered exactly, and the things he did remember were beginning to bother him since he now knew that "the kid" was a real person, Whitney, who was more than just a 1966 unaborted child. It certainly wasn't something he wanted to talk about out loud or even try to recall silently in any detail. Sometimes memory loss was a kind of blessing, "one of God's tender mercies" as his mother would say. It had been three weeks since she'd called. Sam figured it was time to call her.

"The biscuits were good."

"Eva's recipe."

"Yeah, I know. I was just thinking about her. I'm going to call her."

"Be sure and ask about Hazel," Aaron said.

Sam gave him a look of reproach, a "you-don't-have-to-tell-me-what-to-do" look, but he knew it carried no bad feelings. Aaron's tendency to fret over him, especially when it came to amenities, was a running joke.

Sam stretched the phone cord to the bedroom. God, it was a dreadful mess in here. Neither he nor Aaron believed in doing laundry until it became an inescapable chore.

Each ring, whenever he called home, seemed to be especially long and drawn out, as if the telephone itself knew it was Alabama. And Eva never answered quickly.

It didn't matter if she was in the garden or right by the phone, it still took a long time for her to pick up the receiver and say hello.

It rang seven times.

"Hello."

"Mom. Sam."

"I was getting groceries in. Hold it. Let me put the ice cream in the freezer."

Sam looked at his legs. Still Alabama brown. He waited.

"O.K., back," she said. "Have you tried this new soy ice cream?"

"I don't think so."

"Well, they were giving out samples at the store. It tasted all right, so I bought some. Let me get these sandals off. There. Now, how are you?"

"I'm O.K."

"Aaron?"

"Fine. I got a letter from Whitney."

He knew this interested her more than anything he could ever talk about. At last, a girl to talk to his mother about.

"Actually, it was more of a note. She sent some more articles about her father. She wants to get together in November."

"That's good news, don't you think?'"

"Yeah, it's definitely something I want to do."

"Do you want to invite her down?"

"Well, she mentioned me coming to Birmingham."

Eva didn't say anything.

"Of course, if things work out, maybe we could bring her down or something."

"Well, you just do whatever you think is best. Is Aaron going?"

"I haven't thought that through yet. But, anyway, the point is we'll probably be home—there, with you—in early November. And maybe I'll just drive up to Birmingham or something. We'll see."

"O.K., hon."

"How's Hazel?"

Eva's voice changed. "She is very sick. The lungs are going, Sam. You know, those Pall Malls don't help."

"Still smoking, huh?"

"Yes," Eva said, and it made her want one.

"Has she started talking yet?"

"Talking?"

"Talking about dying."

"No."

"Well, follow her lead. But remember, she's going to need to do it, and you're probably the person. She'll be feeling you out, to see if you can handle it."

"Feeling me out?"

"Sure."

"She's the one, though, who's . . ."

"I know, but she'll be handling this better than everyone else, probably. I guess she will. It's usually that way, isn't it?"

"I don't know."

He was getting uncomfortable. Death was one of those things he didn't like to discuss with Eva. It might lead to talking about his father, and there were some things not worth ruining a Saturday morning over.

"Well, anyway, count on us for November if not sooner. Aaron sends his love. We'll make this one short, O.K.?"

"O.K., hon."

He hung up, went back to the kitchen alcove, and got the articles.

At his desk, he studied them in more detail, searching for new ideas. The article said Cal was in favor of the move to take "Onward Christian Soldiers" out of the hymnal because it promulgated war. There was potential here. And this thing about God being a woman —or at least a combination or an interchangeable gender. No, too much there. He wasn't in the mood to work, anyway. He got an envelope, addressed it to Eva, and put the articles in. He had no idea why Whitney kept sending these or why he kept passing them along to his mother.

Eva put the rest of the groceries up and went over to Hazel's. What Sam had told her was fresh on her mind.

She knocked on the jalousie window. Hazel was busy doing something at her office desk, where she kept her metal money box, a pencil, and an ordinary spiral note-book — her appointment book.

"Come in, love."

Hazel's voice was changing. It was raspy.

"You want to go somewhere for lunch?"

Hazel put her pencil aside. Eva tried to avoid peek-ing at what she had been writing.

"We don't need to go anywhere for lunch. Come look."

Eva followed her to the kitchen. A big tray full of cold-cuts was there on the counter.

"I'm not even dead yet, and they're already bringing the food in."

Eva felt something tingly. Was this bait? Like Sam had mentioned? If it was, she surely couldn't bite it.

"Who brought it?"

"The Sunday School class. Who else?"

Eva felt herself tightening. "Looks great," she lied, wondering how she was going to get down this day-of-the-funeral food.

Hazel looked at her watch. "Let's eat," she said. "I was fixing to call you anyway." She got paper plates from the pantry and set the table. "Actually, I think they ordered this from that new deli. Can you imagine Pineapple with a deli? They say it's good, though. We'll see. Don't you think it looks like a deli made it?"

Eva looked it over. The ham, turkey, and roast beef slices were all rolled up. There was a triangle of chicken salad, and one of potato salad, too. The slaw was in a separate pie tin in the center of the tray, topped with lots of black olives.

"O.K., love. Just get a little of everything."

Eva spooned up some chicken salad and slaw. She spread some mayonnaise on bread, unrolled a few pieces of ham, and made a sandwich. She figured a ham sandwich was safe and wouldn't cause her further distress.

Hazel was eating heartily. Eva picked at the chicken salad.

"I was getting the names of my customers together in a long list. I'm going to give them all to that new girl at the Curl Up and Dye. She's a sweet thing, and, God knows, she needs the business. I wanted to get them to her before the next round of x-rays," Hazel said and laughed.

Eva didn't say anything.

"Actually, I was dividing the names into categories—the shampoo-and-set–only ladies, the ones who require twice-a-year perms, the dyes, and that crew of widows who's got to have a new cut, a brand-new look every three months. You know, she might want to pass that last bunch on to someone else. They'll drive you crazy."

Hazel put her hand over Eva's.

"Is something wrong, love?"

"Do you have some milk?"

"Yes. I guess we do need something to drink."

Hazel got the milk from the refrigerator along with two icy glasses. Hazel always kept her glasses in the freezer during summer so they would be ice-cold for the milk.

"Now," she said, sat back down, and continued eating heartily.

Eva picked at her chicken salad some more, and finally put her fork down and said, "Hae. There's no need in me sitting here feeling foolish. We're too old for that. Now, don't laugh at me, O.K.?"

Hazel nodded.

"I was sitting here thinking you might want to talk about dying."

Hazel laughed.

Eva went on, "I was talking to Sam this morning, and he said you might need to talk to somebody, and that somebody might be me."

Hazel took a bite of turkey and cheese. "Well, O.K., just so you can tell Sam we did it. Let's see. I guess my ladies were the main thing, and I've already taken care of that. Or at least the list is made. Now, if I die before tomorrow at noon—that's when I'm taking the list to the Curl Up and Dye—you just run it down to the new girl. Her name is Becky. She has red hair, done in that Dorothy Hamill bob."

Eva smiled and felt her body easing from its tension.

"The will—if you'd call it that—is in my safe deposit box at Alabama Savings and Loan, Selma. My lawyer is Judson Carmichael. Look in the yellow pages. I don't have his number, but he's in Selma, too. I guess he is. I haven't talked to him since I drew up the will, and that was almost ten years ago. He's old."

"O.K.," Eva said.

"I guess that's about it."

"The things in your house. Is there anything special?"

"I'm giving it all to the church."

Eva wondered who was responsible for the business details, but she thought it not right to ask.

"So, that's it," Hazel concluded and got some olives from the tray.

"Are we supposed to talk about how you feel about it?"

"I feel like everything's taken care of, except getting that list over to the redhead."

Eva leaned over the table. "Hazel, you act like you're just going on a little trip."

"Well?" Hazel said.

FOURTEEN

"It's kind of fancy," Mary Ellen said, taking in the crown molding, ceiling fans, and exquisite tile work. "I guess it was just a matter of some simple restoration, though."

Nat was glad he'd thrown on the beige pressed pants and white dress shirt. He glanced at his sleeves, checking for cat hair. He'd asked Mary Ellen to lunch, and he felt self-conscious in this place. It'd been his idea, though, to come here. After all, it was right down from headquarters, in the heart of Five Points, Cal's church was visible, and, from the outside, it hadn't looked so uptown. Then again, he should have known. All the old buildings were being turned into "nice" places to eat, shop, or trade antiques.

"I have mixed feelings," Mary Ellen said. "It's good that the neighborhood is being preserved. I just remember it in the old days. A part of me feels at home in wreckage."

What part is that? Nat wanted to ask her. Instead, he looked at the menu.

"What are you having?" she asked him.

Nat studied the items. "Probably one of these ten-dollar sandwiches."

Mary Ellen smiled.

"I think I'm going to get this pasta salad."

"Let's bill it to the church," Nat said.

"Let's bill it to Albert Naylor," Mary Ellen said. "Or to the INS."

Nat held up a finger. "That's it," he confirmed.

The waitress took their order. They both turned, simultaneously, to the window at their left. The sidewalks were in mint condition, and the city had put up old-fashioned lampposts. "Now, I could do without those," Mary Ellen said, pointing to one. "They're not authentic. I don't like for somebody to try to make something look old."

A mother passed, toting an infant in a kind of papoose sack. There were as many bicycles as cars on the street.

"Have you seen that exercise place on the corner?" Mary Ellen asked him.

"Yeah. Nice place."

She gave him that expectant look—like her face wanted to break into something, maybe a smile. The exercise place was a tiny corner establishment that had been carpeted and painted some pastel Nat couldn't name. There was no furniture, but in the mornings and evenings, you could look in the big window and see young women in leotards of all colors, working out to music.

"I guarantee not a one is a day over twenty-five," Mary Ellen said.

"Too young for me," Nat lied.

"Don't you think our church is in a very strategic location?"

"In terms of the campaign?"

"No, in terms of reaching all kinds of people."

"Oh," he said.

"Well, don't you think so?"

"I guess it is."

Mary Ellen folded her hands on the ivory tablecloth. They reminded Nat of Whitney's hands.

After a long while, too long, Nat thought, the food arrived. Next to his ten-dollar ham sandwich was a concoction he didn't recognize. Mary Ellen eyed it, too. "Um," she said. "I think that's raspberry sauce on the salad."

"Taste it and see," he said. He didn't like to eat anything until he knew first what it was.

Mary Ellen picked up her fork. "Oh, Nat, it's really delicious. Walnuts and bleu cheese on romaine. And that *is* raspberry sauce of some kind."

"Why don't you eat it," he said. "Here." And he began spooning it onto Mary Ellen's bread dish.

"You don't want it?"

"No. I can assure you, I don't."

He looked at her pasta salad. It looked awful. The pasta was a lot of different colors—peagreen, pink, yellow.

"What year did you and Cal come to this place? The church, I mean."

"Let's see, we took this church in 1971."

"You took it?"

Mary Ellen waved it away. "That's just something we say. 'We took it' just means that's when we took the job of pastoring it."

"Oh."

"Before that, we were moving all over Alabama, taking these little country churches. It was something, let me tell you."

Nat took the beansprouts and parsley off his sandwich.

"You don't want those beansprouts?"

"No."

"They're loaded with B vitamins. That bunch there would have something like a thousand times the RDA.

"You want them?"

"No," she said and laughed. "I think they taste terrible."

"What were you saying, about the country churches?"

"Oh, you can imagine. It was late sixties. I was this self-appointed social worker, and Cal was trying to integrate. It was a mess."

"Yeah, Cal told me about that guy punching him out at a revival for trying to let blacks in."

"He loves that story," Mary Ellen said.

"What were y'all like then?" Nat asked.

"What do you mean?"

Nat wasn't sure what he meant. He took a bite of his sandwich and didn't say anything.

Mary Ellen reached over and touched his sleeve. "Seriously, what did you mean?"

"I'm not sure," he said.

"Well, what were *you* like?" she asked him.

"I was in high school," he said.

"Oh, you babe."

"I guess the ten years that separate us—me from you and Cal..."

She was nodding her head. "Yes, it was probably a big gap back then," she said. She folded her hands in a kind of firm, businesslike fashion. "I think I know what you're asking. What were we like politically, and how did we have fun within the necessary boundaries of our profession?"

"Yes."

"If I showed you pictures of us, you would think we looked like everybody else looked. Cal's hair was long, we wore torn-up jeans and sandals. As far as fun goes," she stopped and looked out the window, "we didn't have fun." Nat studied her classic profile. "You were probably a part of the frolicking caboose," she said. "My guess is that you got the sex and drugs—without the burdens."

"What were the burdens?"

"Oh, that's a heavy-handed word. Whitney hates for me to use that word. They were all so self-imposed. I guess they still are," she said.

She leaned closer, playing with her fork. "I will tell you, though, there were lots of people in our profession who used those encounter group things for fun."

"I've never been in one. Are they fun?"

"What I mean is that they provided a 'safe' arena for getting physical with other people. Understand?"

"Yeah, I do."

"Well," she said, leaned back, and pushed the sleeves of her bright canary-yellow shirt up her bronzed arms. "I've done all the talking. We're here on business, aren't we?" She smiled her wife-of-a-pastor-running-for-Congress smile and got out her American Express card.

"I'm paying," Nat reminded her.

She shook her head.

"Come on," he said.

"O.K., let's settle it later. Let's have some coffee now," she said.

Nat flagged the waitress, and ordered two cappuccinos.

He pulled his chair up as close as it'd go to the table. "I want to talk to you about two things. One is Cal. The other is the month of September."

Mary Ellen nodded.

"Is he doing better?"

Mary Ellen picked up her fork again and fingered

the prongs. "He's still feeling..." She paused. "Yes, he is better."

Nat looked at her hard.

"Really, I believe he's feeling better."

"I mean, he's over this deportation thing?"

"It's not a *thing*, Nat."

"I'm sorry, I'm sorry. I didn't mean to be brusque."

"See, there's something you don't understand. You've probably had some very regrettable things happen in your life, haven't you? I mean, like things you've done to hurt people—when you were drunk or living loose or in the midst of hedonist pursuits of some kind. Things that would make this—by 'this,' I mean Cal's running for Congress and causing the investigation and deportation to happen—things that would make this seem very tame and uneventful. But, you've got to understand that, to Cal, this is probably one of the worst things that he's ever done."

Nat considered this. He knew he had probably hurt people, but it wasn't, he felt, as a result of hedonistic living. He knew he was, in some way, a disappointment to his father and grandfather because he didn't go the way they wanted. He didn't go to law school. He had finished up at the University, finally, with a degree in Urban Studies. He hadn't actually *hurt* his parents. And last night he'd had dinner with his father, who was obviously heartened, pleased, down-right proud, Nat felt, about Nat managing Cal's campaign. It was, after all, a *big deal*. This might be the thing that erased any lingering disappointment. And, if Cal won, there was just no telling what might happen. There were possibilities too good to imagine. Washington. He'd only been there once, by train, with his eighth-grade class. That was in 1965.

"What are you thinking?" Mary Ellen asked him.

Nat turned to her. She was smiling that radiant, painful smile, as if she knew all of his thoughts.

He hesitated.

"I'm wondering who I've hurt."

Mary Ellen touched his hand. "Maybe you haven't, Nat."

Her soft hand lay over his. Her wedding ring was only a very thin gold band. No diamond.

"Do you think disappointing people is the same as hurting them?"

"Who are you thinking about?"

"My father. Grandfather. Maybe my mother."

"You've disappointed them?"

"Not really," he said.

She lifted her hand from his.

"What about women?" she asked him.

"Somebody always gets hurt in a relationship, don't they?"

Mary Ellen shrugged. "Has that been your experience?"

Nat looked out the window. The traffic light changed from red to green, and a stream of cars crossed the intersection. His experience had been that falling in love is better than being in love. Marriage was a foreign and slightly distasteful thought—kind of like imagining his parents in bed. And he knew he wasn't good at being faithful. And the truly unsettling thing was that running a campaign, especially this campaign, carried more passion than any sex he'd ever had. The way he felt about Whitney, and Cal and Mary Ellen for that matter, fueled him with something stronger than love and certainly more intense than desire. This was, he guessed, what most people called romance.

"What is it?" Mary Ellen said. He turned from the window to face her. It was tempting—to tell her things, but she was part of the whole picture, and there was no point in putting everything on the table. There was never any point in that.

"Cal is staying in the race, isn't he?" he asked her.

Mary Ellen turned to the window again. "I believe

so," she said. "If you'd asked me that four days ago, I'd have said no. I had some serious doubts right after we found out about Rosa."

"O.K. You keep me posted."

"Right," she said, smiled, and studied his face searchingly. "I take it that you are—that a campaign manager is—a kind of broker/agent/psychiatrist all embodied in one person."

"You got it."

"You know, I've had some strong and interesting feelings about you."

Nat looked at her.

"It's as if you are taking my place."

"Your place?"

"I take care of Cal."

"You do?" he said in mock surprise.

She grinned.

"Do you think most women do that? Take care of men?" she asked.

"I don't know."

"I think you *take charge* better than I do," she said.

"Taking charge is good for a campaign. I doubt if it's good for a marriage, but then I've never been married."

Mary Ellen stared out the window pensively.

"I feel that we should be paying you," she said. "You know, it's hard to believe that somebody would give all this time, every waking moment, to the campaign, to our campaign. It creates quite a feeling of humility and gratitude." She put a nail to her lips, and Nat felt, for a moment, that she was going to get teary.

"I don't spend every waking moment. I still go to work, you know. Every day, seven to three."

"I forget that," she said. "I forget you have a job. What do you do out there, anyway?"

"Right now, I'm operating a furnace, but I've done a little bit of everything over the years," he told her. It was always strange trying to describe work to somebody who had never been in the plant. "I welded a while. Millwright. Electrical. Maintenance jobs pay better than production in terms of hour base, but then there's the bonus with production."

Mary Ellen leaned forward. "I thought you had to go to school to learn how to weld or be an electrician."

"Yes."

"So did they teach you those things in your Urban Studies curriculum?"she asked him with a grin.

"Hardly," he said and smiled.

She looked at him quizzically. "Then how did you learn?"

"You can learn a lot watching other people work."

There just wasn't a nice, modest way to tell her that he could do absolutely anything in the plant. There was no way to tell her that he was good at everything and knew almost instinctively how to do anything he'd ever tried.

"So you run a furnace now?"

"It's called q-bop. It's new. That's why I changed to production. I like something new, you know."

"Yes, I think I know that about you."

"And, there's the team incentive in production. It's not a one-man show. You can see that I'd like that, too."

"Yes."

She picked up her spoon and turned it over. "Have you ever considered," she stopped and looked him in the eye, "I hope this won't offend you. Have you ever considered getting into management? Leaving the Union?"

Of course he had. It was a heady thing to think about. Management had put out their feelers before whenever there was a good opening, and he'd always given them the message that, no, he wasn't interested. To Mary Ellen, he said, "I would be giving up a lot if I ever did that."

"What?"

He shrugged. "I'd give up my office."

Nat knew he was the youngest man ever to hold the vice-president position with Local 431.

"So you'd be giving up power."

He smiled at her. "Right."

"Hardly worth it, huh?"

He feared there was an edge of disdain in her voice, and that immediately disturbed him.

"It's more than that," he said.

She put her hand over his once again. "Is this hard for you to talk about?"

He looked at her, felt her hand. He wished there were more women like her in the world.

"So what are the components of your discomfort?" she pursued.

"It would have ramifications," he said. "It would be a career crisis."

She leaned back. "So," she said, "you can truly understand what Cal is going through—imagining yourself making a change like that."

"Of course."

It was more than that, though. It would be saying that he was choosing to look at the world in a different way. He would be, as his mother had pled with him in the past, using his degree, as if a front-line supervisor in steel-making uses a degree in Urban Studies. It would be, in his father's eyes, the return of the prodigal son. It just wasn't worth thinking about now, and anyway, if Cal won, none of this would matter. The career change this might lead to for Nat was too sweeping to believe.

"Listen, September will be crazy," he said.

She turned from the window.

"It will be busy. That's when all the TV stuff will happen. I want you to know what's coming. It will be good—the TV coverage will—for the campaign." Nat finished up his coffee. "You look good on camera."

"Oh, we all do, don't we? Cal and Whitney and me."

"Yeah, you do. You were made for this," he said seriously.

"I'm afraid we all know that. All too well."

Nat nodded. "Cal and I have talked about it—the camera ease."

"We know it's something we have to fight."

"Why fight it? Why fight the knowledge that you're appealing and people like to look at you and listen to you? I don't understand that. I don't understand that way of thinking."

"It's not godly," she said evenly. "It spells disaster. Look at TV evangelists. Do you consider most of them godly?"

She had a point. "It's not the same," he argued.

"No?" She raised an eyebrow. She looked for all the world like Whitney when she did it.

"I guess you have to separate the campaign from the ministry. He's running for Congress, and the media is part of it. It's not like he's using media for his ministry."

Mary Ellen looked at him. "Cal is changing careers. That's very stressful."

Nat nodded.

"Especially since it's all up in the air. This district will determine whether or not Cal will actually change careers. It's his desire to change that disturbs him."

"A disturbed man makes a shaky candidate."

He feared this statement might make her mad, but it was something he'd needed to say for a long time. Instead, though, it caused her shoulders—clad in their tropical yellow attire—to fall into what looked like comfort. "Yes, I agree," she said. "Lucky he has us to doctor up his disturbances." She smiled. Nat believed it was a sincere smile and statement. "I really do want to pay for this," she said, gesturing to the empty plates.

"Listen, I need to ask you one more thing," he said.

"O.K." She held her American Express card in her palm.

"Why did you adopt Whitney?"

She gave him a mischievous look. "We wanted to have children."

He felt foolish, but then she put her hand over his. "I was a DES baby."

Nat looked at her. He knew vaguely what this meant.

"My mother took DES when she was pregnant with me."

"Well, Whitney is something else," he said, feeling the color flood his face.

"Yes. It was relatively easy to adopt, for us it was. Hannah Home, where she was born, was right there by Ft. McClellan when we were stationed there. And, you know, it being a Christian home, Cal being a chaplain . . ."

Nat took out his VISA, and Mary Ellen shook her head. They fenced for a while with their credit cards, and finally Nat won. He paid, but on the bottom of the check, he wrote, "Bill to INS."

Whitney rode with Nat to pick up the yard signs and the posters. They circled over the mountain and into the zoo entrance. The August heat was becoming a kind of joke. July's onslaught of humidity and hundred-degree marks was terribly unsettling, like a first wave of nausea, but now everybody was resigned to misery. Here in Nat's compact car, though, it was cool. Whitney felt real good. Going to the zoo to pick up posters that read "Calvin Gaines for Congress" was, itself, a remarkably funny thing to be doing on a Saturday morning in hundred-degree heat. Whitney was fond of bizarre things. Nat stopped the car by a fence on the far left side of the zoo. Behind it were the zebras and kangaroos. A peacock screamed. Whitney looked over at Nat. He was grinning. One thing she knew: She and Nat shared a longing for things out of the ordinary, and this was right down their alley.

"Francy said Yarbrough's house was on this side," he said.

"We need a map of the zoo," Whitney thought and then said it.

Nat looked at her. "I doubt seriously if the Birmingham Zoo has maps. It's kind of small, don't you think?"

"It was always big enough for me."

"Me, too. I think we should get out and walk back through those pines."

Whitney put her tennis shoes back on, and they got out and walked. The smell of animals was in the air.

"Can you imagine living here?" Nat asked her.

"Yes."

He looked at her. "You'd like that, wouldn't you?"

"Wouldn't you?"

"Francy says Yarbrough founded a nudist camp in north Alabama," Nat said.

Whitney laughed.

"Do you believe it?" he asked her.

"Francy never lies."

Whitney waved the insects from her eyes. The pines opened up, and Yarbrough's house appeared. It was built of logs and stone. They ascended the steps. On the front porch, there were some big boxes with the words, "Gaines Posters" printed on them. A big note was taped to one. Nat and Whitney read it together. "Baby gorilla born this morning at 7! Gone to help Mama recupe. Here are posters. Yarbrough."

Whitney wanted to go find the gorilla, but she didn't say so. Instead, she wiped the perspiration drops from her forehead and looked at Nat. As if reading her mind, Nat said, "I wish we had time."

Whitney tried to pick up a box. It was too heavy.

Nat put one hand in his jeans pocket, and ran the other through his hair. Whitney knew this meant he was considering his next move. She'd grown to recognize his patterns and gestures and understood them intimately. He was like a member of the family, but she did not know how to categorize him. This kind of confusion was troubling but arousing. Whitney liked to fit people and feelings into compartments. Nat didn't fit. She watched him and followed the motions of his hand, moving over the dark locks. One thing she often imagined herself doing was touring the steel plant, coming up on him unexpectedly, catching him in the process of doing whatever steelworkers did at work. She knew she was curious about the interworkings of his life. Beyond that, she did not understand her feelings. They were one piece of this new kaleidoscope of uncertainties— Nat, Sam, Diana, the campaign, Washington, theater, the future. It was, like most kaleidoscopes, bright and fascinating but unnerving and subject to change.

He caught her eye, and she immediately felt color rising in her face. She'd been studying him too intently and discovered in the act of doing so. For a moment, she feared he was going to kiss her or something. She gave him her full-force Sunday smile to disarm him, and it worked. He disengaged the intense eye contact and his body appeared to retreat, though he'd never really moved at all—either toward her or away from her. It was his look of *imminent* passion that she was responding to, and she carried the visual image of this with her through most of the morning—trying to decide where to file it.

"A baby gorilla was born this morning," she told Francy.

They were at headquarters, opening the boxes of posters and trying to decide where to put them. Francy was doing most of the work, and Whitney was bending her ear with chatter. She knew she was chattering, and she knew it was not something she generally did, but she was always more prone to do it with Francy. Francy was a good listener, and she liked trivia. Whitney felt light-headed and almost happy. Nat had obtained a lot

of new city maps, and she had spent a long time looking at them. Having discovered her love for maps, he'd
put her in charge of locating various streets and neighborhoods all over the district. When the heat broke
later in the day, they were going to drive around and
tack up the posters.

"I could do this forever," she told Francy.

"You and maps," Francy said.

"These are really new," Whitney said. "The one I
have at home isn't anywhere near this complete. See,
that new development out by the Galleria is on here,
even. These are really good maps. See how these streets
and avenues form tiny perfect rectangles. Oh, it's so
fine."

Francy looked up from the boxes. "You know, my
therapist would have some things to say about you."

"Like what?"

"I believe you are obsessive-compulsive."

"What does that mean?"

"A lot of things, but you seem to experience an abnormally great degree of satisfaction in having things
in order. I suspect that you feel threatened, in fact, if
things are not just so."

Whitney smiled at her. Francy's and Mary Ellen's be-
havioral interpretations amused her, but she couldn't
totally discount them because she adored and respected
these two women more than anyone she knew. Francy
was wearing white pants and an aqua one-hundred-
percent-cotton shirt. She wore a sand dollar around
her neck. Her sunglasses were pulled up and perched
in her honey-colored, wavy hair. Her general attire this
morning spelled "Home from the Beach"—though she
had certainly been on no vacation these past few days.

"You know," Francy said, and stood up from the box,
"this is a dangerous-looking object." She held up the
box-opener.

"We're a dangerous bunch," Nat called. He was in the

storeroom, apparently within earshot. "We're sending the country to hell in a hand-basket."

"Yes," Francy called back. "Calvin Gaines is a danger to our children."

Whitney tried to get in on the banter, but this particular political sling of mud always disturbed her. It was so personal and bad, and she didn't fully understand it. She knew it had something to do with allowing children to read whatever books interested them and not having to pray at school and letting women have abortions if they wanted them—even though Cal considered it a sin. Beyond that, it was all a mystery.

Around lunchtime, headquarters began filling up. It was truly astounding, the number of people who appeared, took posters, and disappeared—back to their cars or vans. Coley, the archeologist, arrived at one with his Nigerian student. His rotund, bald head was glistening. He rubbed it. "It's nice to have inherited this particular gene during the dog days of Alabama summer. Glad I left Michigan. Be hard there in winter, all bare up top." His student, whom Whitney had never formally met, stood by his side and smiled first at him, then at Francy, then at Whitney. She was very pleasant-looking and the most serene individual Whitney had ever observed.

Whitney knew it was time to introduce herself.

"I'm Whitney," she said and extended her hand.

The girl took it. "I'm Vashti," she said.

"Thanks for helping," Whitney said.

"I am lucky to have the opportunity to work on an American campaign."

Francy stopped opening boxes. She reached in her aqua shirt pocket and got what Whitney knew was one of Cal's cards.

"Join us some time. You will feel right at home," she said.

Coley looked at the card before handing it to Vashti.

Francy gave Coley a defiant kind of smile, like—Just try to tell me there's something wrong with going to church.

After Coley and Vashti left with armloads of posters and leaflets, Francy said to Whitney, "He's like her bodyguard." Francy tore open the last box, sat on the floor, and wiped her forehead. "Those University people are the most antichurch crew I've ever seen."

"Now, now," Nat said, coming from behind the partition.

"They are," Francy affirmed.

"They're good workers," he reminded her.

"I know, I know. But they ought to support Cal's ministry."

"Isn't that what they're doing now?"

"No. They're supporting his candidacy, not his ministry."

Nat shrugged.

"We believe in separation of church and state, Nathaniel. Don't forget. That's what our conference has been fighting about."

Whitney watched Nat.

He was distracted. He had a pencil behind his ear. He was standing perfectly still, hands on hips, deep in the thoughts of a campaign manager, staring at the opened boxes. He looked up and, again, caught Whitney looking at him. The worried lines on his face began changing to something else—that same look he'd worn at the zoo, the coded look Whitney knew she wasn't ready to decipher. She quickly turned to Francy. "What's next?" she asked.

Francy looked at her watch. "Lunch."

They rode over to the farmer's market cafeteria on the west side—near the steel plant. It was Nat's idea.

"Lots of mixed neighborhoods out this way," he said to Francy.

He turned to Whitney in the back seat. "We'll do well there." Then he added to Francy, "We'll do well everywhere except the snow-white pockets."

Francy pulled her sunglasses down from where they'd been perched in her wavy, honey-colored hair. The sun streamed in from the car's sunroof and fell on Whitney's legs. She'd spent most of the summer indoors, at headquarters. She was wearing earth-colored safari shorts with her fading tan. Two years ago, she wouldn't have been caught dead looking like this.

"Phone banks covered for tonight?" Nat asked Francy.

"That's not my job," she said.

Nat looked over at her. She glanced his way. "Well, it's not," she said.

"O.K., O.K. We need to set up some assistants. Put somebody in charge of phones, posters, media, malls, neighborhoods."

Francy nodded.

"Did you talk to Cal about hitting those black churches in September?"

"I haven't talked any campaign with Cal since you told me not to. When's his sabbatical over anyway? When does he get back in the race?"

Nat turned to Whitney. "How's he doing?"

"I guess I'm his doctor?"

Nat smiled at her, and she turned to the window.

"He's fine, I guess," she said. "He's been spending a lot of time in the backyard. He's been feeding the birds and watering the azaleas."

"Stop here," Nat said.

Francy pulled over. They were entering a west-side neighborhood called Fairfield. "This is where I grew up," he said to Whitney. He got out of the car and raised the hatchback to get some signs, nails, and the hammer. He tacked signs onto telephone poles while Francy drove at a snail's pace alongside him. Whitney liked this. She liked the sight of Nat using a hammer. He got back in the car. "Just wanted the thrill of doing that. It's too hot. This is a night-time job. We'll do more of this tonight." Whitney believed he kind of glanced her way when he said this, but she wasn't sure.

"Is it legal?" Francy asked. "I mean, is it O.K. to drive nails into telephone poles?"

"Everybody does it," Nat replied.

"You didn't answer my question."

"It's easier to get forgiveness than permission. If somebody says anything, we'll quit. It doesn't matter anyway," Nat said. "The Naylor people will be right behind us, taking them down. You know, I was wondering," he said and threw an arm over the back of Francy's seat, "if there are Naylor supporters in your church and, if so, how they're dealing with all this."

"Yeah, we wondered that, too, when we learned we'd been investigated. What do you think?" she asked Whitney in the rearview mirror.

Whitney didn't have any idea. "I don't know," she said. She was getting real hungry. She hoped they were close to the farmer's market.

"You know what gets me the most?" Francy said. "It's this chilling feeling that 'we're it'—I mean you, me, Whitney, we're *it*. All these people are working on this campaign, but you, me, Whitney, Coley, Yarbrough, and those schoolteachers are the core. *We* are sending this man to Washington."

"Oh, I love it," Nat said and hit his fist on the dashboard. "Go America! That's a great grassroots speech, Francy. We need you on TV saying that."

Whitney believed she had heard this before.

"That's the psychology of it," Nat said. "What you're feeling is what all these people will begin to feel, and this realization, this 'I'm responsible' kind of thing is what drives a campaign. Once that takes over the campaign assumes a life of its own, and the mystical has occurred. It's like the formation of a star."

Francy turned to him. "That's the most fanciful thing I've ever heard you say."

"I worked the congressional race last time, too," Nat

said. "It was managed by somebody they brought in from Memphis or Nashville, I can't remember which. That guy was shrewd. He led us to believe that a 'phantom committee' existed—a group of well-known local people who had political muscle—but they couldn't make themselves known because it would jeopardize their careers in some way. We were always under the impression that this phantom committee was fueling the campaign, financially or in some other vague ways we didn't exactly understand. All this was so we would feel that this was the right candidate to support, that we were not alone, that there was some higher power over us and blessing our work."

"Sounds like one of Cal's opening vignettes," Francy noted.

"Well, it worked. It was enticing, trying to imagine who these people were and why they must remain anonymous. Of course, we lost."

"Yes. It was a shame. People just didn't pay attention to what was happening."

"They will this time," Nat said.

FIFTEEN

Eva knelt by Sam, Sr.'s, grave, pulling up weeds and nutgrass. She hadn't been here since Memorial Day when she placed the traditional fruit jar—filled with roses, hydrangea, or whatever was in bloom—beside his grave. She gazed over to the pasture adjacent the graveyard by the church where she observed dinner-on-the-grounds every year after tidying up his grave. Always, there were other widows doing the same thing, so it wasn't a sad occasion—just another domestic duty, a kind of after-the-fact spring cleaning. But today, it was another story. There were no other widows.

Everybody had already left Hazel's graveside service. Eva wasn't sure why she kept hanging around Sam's place. When he first died, she felt he was in the stars, light-years gone. She'd send long-distance messages into the sky. Now, he felt as nearby as the marker itself, but she didn't know what to say.

"Hazel died," she said to the marker that read, "Samuel Kirby, Born 1919, Died 1965." She waited. She looked around for a sign. The air was hot and still.

"You're not listening, are you, Sam? Nothing new, huh?" She smiled at the marker.

"I'm considering striking up a friendship with the redhead at Curl Up and Dye. Do you think that odd?"

Eva felt her body weakening in the midday heat, but she didn't care. She looked to the left and right. "I hope there's room for me," she said. "This place is filling up." And, to herself, she added, I'd hate to be buried in Awin or Furman or Snowhill or, God forbid, Selma.

She turned her attention back to Sam, Sr.'s, marker. "You wouldn't believe," she said. She wasn't sure what she wanted to say. How on earth to fill Sam in on twenty years since he'd been gone. He'd never believe the changes. Somebody had told her—it was the daughter of one of Hazel's customers, who had a fresh degree in psychology and probably wasn't a reliable source of newly discovered truths—this young woman had told her that there was an abnormally high number of psychiatric hospital admissions and suicides in Alabama among white males after the Selma–Montgomery march. She, herself, in fact, was treating a man who had been taking Thorazine since 1965. He had been in the National Guard and had seen his first angel marching right alongside Dr. King on the Edmund Pettus Bridge. Eva felt there was absolutely no correlation, though, between historical events and Sam's death. He was simply destined genetically, she believed, to lose his mind in 1965.

And it wasn't the social changes, anyway, that would be so riveting to Sam. It was Eva herself. She knew that his death had caused a dramatic shuffling of the cards. She almost considered herself the survivor of a closed-head injury. She'd heard that accidents of this nature can create a new personality—the trauma is so profound—and often the new formation is delightfully better than what existed prior to impact. She considered herself in this vein—a new person, a woman with a peculiarly strong and happy heart.

It had not always been so. Prior to her "injury," she recalled herself as having been kind of bewildered and uneasy with the business of living. Death frightened her, and she was prone to a kind of irrational, magical thinking—like if she didn't stack the linens in a certain way, it might cause some unforeseen accident to occur. Or, if she used one towel and not the other, it might hurt the other's feelings. She'd never told anyone these things, and she feared it bordered on the kind of thing that sent a person to seek the services of someone like Hazel's customer's daughter. And she spent a lot of time in wistful daydreaming. The sight of a sheet, hanging from the clothesline, suddenly caught up in a spring breeze was enough to bring her to tears. She arranged flowers, and although she was quite skilled and often won blue ribbons in the shows up in Selma, there was something (she felt now, in retrospect) almost tragic in the way she labored over the arc of a crabapple branch or the placement of color. She felt affection for her former self, but she knew this person was ill-equipped to deal with the reality of the world. She did not consider herself bitter or hard; indeed, she would have been had she not undergone the metamorphosis after Sam's death. The former Eva would never have been able to build good knee calluses, win the battle with dandelions, or love Aaron. Overall, she'd felt lucky. Until today. "Until this very moment," she said aloud to Sam's marker.

"And why's that?" she asked for him, since he wasn't saying much.

She looked up at the green canopy by Hazel's gravesite. She believed that she'd loved Hazel more than she'd loved Sam. But, then, it was hard to say. Sam had been gone for twenty years, and Hazel only one day. To love someone you're not bound to by blood or marriage is a kind of miracle, Eva thought.

"I don't even know that redhead," she said to Sam. "I've seen her, but I don't know her."

Eva got up from her kneeling position, brushed the grass from her legs and dress, then walked to her station wagon. She dreaded going home. The church women, not knowing where else to take the food since Hazel had no kin, had brought it all to Eva's house that morning. Hazel's closest friends had eaten lunch there, at Eva's, some of them taking their plates over to Hazel's yard, to the folding chairs by the pecan tree. Now Eva must face the day-of-the-funeral cuisine, leftovers no less. This was the kind of thing she and Hazel would joke about, and she was certain—as certain as her spiritual side would blessedly allow—that Hazel was alive somewhere, laughing at Eva's predicament with the food. The problem was, Hazel wasn't *here* to share in the mirth. "Where are you, Hae?" When she said it, she felt a tingly sensation, and, for a moment, she thought the sunlight did something funny, a kind of shimmying thing, accompanied by a voice—an incredible contralto holding one vibrant note. When it was over, she longed to believe it had actually happened. She could almost accept it, but she understood that early grief carried these kinds of hallucinatory overtones.

It was October first, and the heat wasn't anywhere near leaving. True, the sun fell in a different slant, coming on her at an angle she liked, but it was no less hot for its gradual shift. Eva parked the station wagon in her driveway, got out, and stood against the car door, keys in hand. Hazel's place was, naturally, just the same. This thing about death had always gotten to her—the way nothing else changes. It was like Hazel should have taken her house, her shop, with her rather than leaving it here to remind Eva of its emptiness. Was this supposed to be anger she was feeling? She didn't care for all the death literature these days—all the stages she was, according to the death experts, going to have to go through before she "accepted" Hazel's being gone, as if you could ever *accept* somebody dying, as if it's some kind of gift or something. She went over to Hazel's yard and ran her fingers along the scaley-bark hickory tree. This thing lives, Eva thought, and Hazel dies. This tree that's destined to become somebody's snow-skis someday gets to live. She wasn't sure if that was true or not about the scaley-bark wood being used for skis. A man she'd met on the oncology unit in Selma had told her this sometime during early September when Hazel got real sick and the spot on the liver appeared. Eva and this man—his name was Herb—were sitting on a patio of sorts they'd built on the hospital's new wing. You stepped out the surgery/oncology waiting-room door to this patio that was actually on top of the lower roof. There were some plants, wrought-iron furniture, and multicolored gravel that formed tiny paths that led nowhere. It was intended, she supposed, as a quiet place for a family member to come for fresh air, a place landscaped with good intentions, its design attempting to say, Casual, Natural, Just Another Normal Day— reinforcing the family's cancer denial. So Eva and Herb struck up a conversation here in the wrought-iron chairs, kind of aimlessly kicking gravel. His wife was dying. "She probably won't make it through the month," he'd told Eva.

"You got family here?" he asked.

"Friend."

"Umm."

"*Good* friend."

"I hear you," he said.

Herb had a gray moustache, but his hair was brown. Probably dyed, Eva thought. He had deep indentations on his face that weren't necessarily scars, just marks. He told her he'd been to Chicago recently and had seen an exhibit of totem poles in a museum there. "Each carving on a pole represents a life event," he said. Eva listened with interest. "One man's pole had a child being devoured by an animal. That kind of got to me, you know." When he said that, his eyes locked with Eva's. The scars and lines on his face suddenly took on special meanings like the carvings he was describing, and Eva knew that already his wife's pending death had begun to etch itself along his brow. She died two weeks later, and Eva didn't see Herb again.

Hazel went quietly. On the eve of the actuality, she asked Eva to sing. "Oh Hae, I hate to sing," she said and smiled.

"I know, love. It's the only good thing about dying. You can ask outrageous favors of your friends."

It was their last joke.

The rest was all morphine, machines, and Eva's songs. The numbers on the monitors let Eva know that Hazel was dying.

Now, she ran her fingers once more over the scaley-bark hickory then went inside. It was warm. She turned on the window unit, got the iced-tea pitcher from the refrigerator, and drank a glass. Then she went to the phone and called Sam's number. Aaron answered.

"Sam's out with friends. You O.K.?"

"Not really, she said.

"The graveside service. Was it, ah, comforting?"

"Not especially," she said. She sat on the red stool and idly drummed her fingers on her recipe box. "They read the thirteenth chapter of First Corinthians, that thing about love. Brother Ed gave her eulogy— real factual, light on the sweet details he might have included if he had a better way with words. I don't know, Aaron, there's no way to eulogize Hazel."

"I understand," he said.

"You do, huh?"

Eva looked out the window at the hickory. "I'm seriously considering making a totem pole," she said.

"Did you say a totem pole?"

"Yes."

"That's an unusual thing to do."

"Is it? I need to carve Hazel into wood."

"Are you O.K., Eva?"

"No. This is an awful day."

"What're you going to do tonight?"

Eva looked around her kitchen. "I don't know. The place is spotless. I've got all this funeral food to dispose of somehow."

"Well, can you eat it?"

"Maybe I'll freeze these casseroles. I wish you and Sam were here to help me eat everything."

"We'll be there next month."

She looked at her calendar. She'd circled the second week in November.

"That's almost six weeks away."

"Do you want us to come sooner? Do you want Sam to fly home now, tomorrow? He can, I'm sure."

It was a very alluring idea. "No," she said.

"Will you call us if you need us?"

"O.K., hon," she said, but she knew she'd never do it.

When they hung up, she picked up her sandals and carried them to her bedroom closet. It was dark and smelled of cedar.

Aaron went to Sam's desk and got a sheet of paper. He'd never meddled in Sam's or Eva's or anyone else's life. Not meddling was something his parents had taught him with vegeance. It presented professional conflicts, since he was a social worker and his daily agenda involved endless acts of intervention into other people's lives. He avoided family therapy at all costs. He did great assessments, gathering information with care, precision, and a diagnostic eye, but he'd always then pass the case on to a colleague. "This is beyond my realm of expertise," he'd lie to avoid further violation of a family's private arena of dysfunction. This evening, though, he knew it was right to do what he was going to do.

In his letter to Whitney, he told her his reason for writing was to tell her that Eva, her grandmother, was having a hard go of it because her friend and neighbor, Hazel, had died. He thought she, Whitney, might want to know, might even want to write her.

SIXTEEN

Nat stood at the back of the Sixteenth Street Baptist Church. The service had been finished for well over thirty minutes, but the congregation—black men and women dressed with flair—mingled and laughed in festive, celebratory fashion as if in the midst of a holiday party. Most were clustered by the altar where Cal stood shaking hands, all smiles, in his dark-blue suit, white shirt, and red tie. This was vintage Cal, Nat thought. The pianist, a huge, happy, black man, was playing a medley of all the songs from the preceding service, a

kind of musical grand finale. Occasionally, he played
with his right hand only, using his left to wipe the sweat
from his forehead with a big handkerchief. Nat had
been, and still was, swept up in a strange wave of anguished joy. Naturally, the history of this place was a
contributing factor. He was eleven when the church
was bombed, the same age as one of the girls killed.
What he recalled most vividly was that it was the only
time he ever saw his father cry. But it was more than
this particular church. It was Cal himself. During all of
September, Nat had been chauffeuring his candidate to
black churches, listening to the amens and the wailing
choirs, and knowing these people were marveling that
a white man could preach like this. Cal's passion wasn't
a matter of voice pitch, it was one of remarkably acces-
sible eloquence. The anguished part of Nat's joy was
that he was beginning to fear that Cal belonged here, in
church, and not in Washington. And he believed that
Cal was on his way to Washington. The local pollsters
had him in the lead. Nat feared that he, Nat, was
spearheading a great mistake.

"I think the campaign is making me crazy," he told
Francy later that day. They were in her sunroom. Her
purple-caged lovebirds were making him crazy, too.

"Did I ever tell you I'm afraid of birds?" he asked
her.

Francy smiled in a tender way. "Afraid of birds?"

"Pet store birds."

"Oh."

"Parrots, especially. The kind that sit, uncaged, on
perches in stores."

"Nothing a little desensitization therapy couldn't fix."
She gestured to her lovebirds. "Would you be more
comfortable if I took Nicki and Celeste to another
room?"

"Yes."

Francy picked up the purple cage and went to the
kitchen. "Coffee?" she called.

"Yes. Thanks."

Nat looked around the room. It was only the second time he'd been here. The other time, Whitney had been here, too, and he hadn't been conscious of any of his surroundings—other than her. Now, he noticed that all the sunroom furniture was wicker. The plants were healthy and placed unobtrusively. A lot of women he knew had sunrooms where the plants threatened to eat you alive. Now that the birds were gone, he began to feel his tension easing up. His wicker chair was wide and roomy with a soft light-blue cushion. All of Francy's apartment was subdued. He imagined some therapist telling her, "Paint your house pastels; it will help you relax."

Francy returned with the coffee.

"Church was something this morning," he told her.

She sat in the opposite wicker chair and readjusted her light-blue cushions. The cups and saucers had tiny birds painted on them. Nat gestured to them and smiled.

"Would you like a plain mug?" she asked him.

"No, this is fine. They look like outdoor birds."

Francy sipped her coffee and stared out the big window to Highland Avenue below. Her apartment building was old and antebellum-looking. It had a Birmingham historical marker in the yard. It was a nice place.

"So, tell me about Sixteenth Street Baptist," she said.

"Have you ever been inside it?" he asked her.

"Lots of times."

"Well, I'd never been in there. It got me."

"Yeah. It's something."

"I've been having some bad thoughts," he said.

Francy looked at him.

"Are we doing the right thing?"

"What do you mean?" she asked, leaning forward.

"Should Cal be running?"

Francy put her hands over his. "You've been with Cal too much," she said.

Nat understood what she meant. Late August and early September had been trying. Ten days after Rosa and Mita and Carlos were deported, the INS appeared at the Baldwins', Freemans', and Turners'. Neither Nat nor Cal had talked with anyone, but Francy had taken a call at the church office from an agent who informed her that nothing further would happen provided the church stopped their activities. The three families involved had been visited one by one, and, each time, Cal dropped one degree lower into despondency. Nat had to nurse him back each time, and it hadn't been easy. The Sunday mornings at the black churches had been the saving grace. These services appeared to bring Cal back to life. But the bad thing was that they were having the opposite effect on Nat. They were causing him to doubt the campaign. He was trying to explain this to Francy.

"If you're worried that Cal belongs *here,* you've got to remember that he will still be here. He may not be here geographically, but he'll still be among the people here because he'll be representing them."

"But the church? What will happen to the church?"

Francy smiled, obviously amused. "Are you being saved?" she asked him.

"Don't be ridiculous," he said.

"O.K., just asking, that's all."

"What does that mean, anyway? Are *you* saved?"

"Sure."

"Is Whitney?"

"I would imagine. You'd have to ask her, though."

"Yeah, I'll do that."

"Don't expect a straight answer," Francy said.

"Is she deliberately that way?"

"Oh, I don't think so, Nat. She's just young."

He didn't need to be reminded of that.

"And probably uncertain about a lot of things," Francy added. "It's been a big year for her."

"The campaign?" he asked.

"Well, yes, but she's also real preoccupied with her father, not Cal, the other one."

"She talks to you about things?"

"She talks to me and to Mary Ellen probably more than she talks to most people. Still, I can't say I know her intimately. Maybe she talks to God."

Nat looked out the window. "Yeah, well, they would get along great. He's just as inaccessible as she is."

"Oh, Nat, God's not inaccessible. Go look for him in the stars and trees. Or in Mary Ellen's face. You're not going to find him in your *brain*."

"Who says I'm looking?"

"Everybody is looking."

Nat looked closely at Francy's face. He believed she might actually be fleshing out a little.

"Are you gaining weight?"

Francy changed her body's position in the light-blue cushions. "I can't discuss my weight with anybody but my therapist."

"Now, what kind of bullshit is that?"

Francy looked at her watch. "You want to head on over to headquarters? The meeting's in forty-five minutes."

Nat drained his cup and set it in the saucer. Francy went to the kitchen, got the bird cage, and returned it to the usual spot in the sunroom. "Nicki, Celeste," she said. "This big steelworker is scared of you." Then to Nat, she said, "You're not so big, though, are you?"

He was five-foot-nine. Francy was, it seemed to him, near his height.

"Do you want to ride with me?" he asked her.

She hesitated, finger on lips. "Hmm. No. I need a car there. Well, no, Whitney can bring me home. Sure. I'll ride with you."

In the car, Francy said, "Mary Ellen's doing a great

job, filling in for Cal. She's some kind of preacher—all that signing while she talks."

"Yeah, I bet."

"Is this black church tour over now?"

"Yes. There's one thing you can be sure of. The black vote is all wrapped up."

"Well, that's no surprise, is it?"

"No. It's just a matter now of not publicizing that fact."

Nat pulled into the twenty-four-hour donut shop where Francy had taken him the Sunday he went to church with her.

"Good idea," she said.

"How many do you want?" he asked.

"Five."

He looked at her incredulously. "That's wonderful," he praised.

"O.K., O.K. Don't make a big deal out of it. It's all a delicate balance. And don't ask me to explain that."

At headquarters, things were very busy. Whitney and some men Nat didn't recognize—probably church deacons—were toting folding chairs into the building from somebody's station wagon. Nat had called a general meeting for everybody involved and concerned with the campaign.

"Where did you get all these?" Nat asked Whitney, pointing to the chairs.

"Church."

"Well, that's great."

He began shaking hands with the men, introducing himself, trying to file their names in his head.

"The chairs have *got* to go in a circle," Francy told him.

"There's not enough room for that. They need to be in rows."

"Like a classroom?" she asked.

"Yes."

"Nat, it's better to have a circle. There's a psychology

to it. People need to see each other's faces."

"This isn't group therapy."

She looked hurt by this statement. "O.K.," he conceded. "Put them in a circle." He turned to Whitney. "We're going to have a circle meeting." She smiled at him, and he felt himself melting. It was definitely getting worse.

Nat went to the storeroom to get the remainder of the leaflets and a new notepad. When he returned to the big room, the circled chairs were all taken, and people were still coming in the door.

Francy approached him. "You were right," she said. "Not enough space." Then she moved close to his ear. "I never dreamed there'd be this many."

Nat and Whitney began politely to ask the seated workers to get up so that they might rearrange the chairs to accommodate more people.

"Where're those men?" he asked Whitney. She went to the window.

"They're still here. More chairs?"

"Yes. A lot more."

Whitney went outside. In a while, the men returned with another station-wagon-full of metal folding chairs.

"O.K.," she said to Nat. "This is all of Fellowship Hall. No more chairs."

"It's enough," he said.

Coley came in with a big cake that had "Calvin Gaines for Congress" printed decoratively on the top. It was red, white, and blue.

"Oh, that's so sweet," Francy whispered to Nat. "I shouldn't have talked so disparagingly about him the other day."

Coley was greeted warmly by the others. "We found this in some ruins over on the west side," he said, nodding to the cake.

The chairs were now all lined up, classroom-style, and Nat stood at the front, surveying the workers. Yarbrough had brought his daughters, it appeared, and

Nat saw that Whitney was introducing herself. He imagined she was inquiring about the baby gorilla who had upstaged the campaign in local news, appearing on the front page of the paper in a disposable diaper, generally posed with one of his around-the-clock nurses from Children's Hospital. The schoolteachers were, as usual, clustered together, looking healthy but kind of loony. There were a lot of black ministers, still clad in formal Sunday morning attire; some University professors Coley had recruited, looking hung-over and confused; his Local 431 Union buddies, looking just great; and a potpourri of District 6 people, virtually all ages. It was incredible. This was the thing that kept him perpetually on somebody's campaign trail.

First, he drew some diagrams and figures on the board. Then he introduced Coley and Yarbrough and a guy named Brad Farrow. He described their roles and functions and added that Farrow was treasurer. He was a CPA with a big firm housed in the new Southtrust Bank Building, but Nat didn't mention that. Then he recognized Kiley, the dentist, and Ratliff, the attorney, whose building they were operating from. Then he talked about neighborhoods, phone banks, and the need for typists to address envelopes. He asked if everybody present had a yard sign in his or her yard. He talked about radio spots and TV ads. He lied about how little money they had to work with (Cal's more wealthy church members had fueled them financially) and how this was truly a grassroots campaign where every person mattered. Then, with Francy's help, he divided the whole room into groups based on their zip codes, so that the neighborhood door-to-door could begin. Afterwards, they all ate Coley's patriotic cake and drank coffee. Francy propped the door open to let in the October coolness that had finally arrived. It had the desired effect, and Nat sensed the mass happiness growing, essential to a solid campaign. Gradually, they began filtering out, leaflets in hand, toting big yard signs and hammers and nails donated (though he wished to remain anonymous) by the owner of the Five Points Hardware Store. Eventually, the room was empty except for Nat, Francy, Whitney, and Yarbrough and his daughters. One looked ten maybe, the other was a teenager. Something about the teenager kept bothering him, or at least, he felt himself drawn to look at her. After they left, Whitney asked him, "Did you see her tattoos?"

"Was that it?"

Whitney looked at him quizzically.

"I mean, I knew there was something about her."

"She had a bunch of chrysanthemums growing up from her shirt onto her neck. It was hard to see unless you looked closely. She showed me the whole thing. She had a little rose on her ankle, too. She was kind of a neat person."

"Tattoos. I don't think I've ever seen tattoos on a woman."

Nat glanced around. Francy was gone. Whitney sat on top of the desk, dangling her legs over the side. She was wearing another long dress, but this one looked contemporary, he believed, though he hadn't, up to this point in life, kept abreast of the fashions of teenage girls.

"She got the tattoos in Germany. She went there last summer with a cycling group. Have you ever been out of the country?"

"No," he said. "Have you?"

"No."

He pulled up a chair and looked at her dangling feet. She was wearing blue sandals that reminded him of Francy's wicker furniture.

"You want to know something? I've never been out of the South," he told her.

She looked at him. "Neither have I. My birth father lives in New York, you know. Do you think I'll ever go there?"

"How could I possibly know the answer to that?"

Her face fell. For a moment, she looked like she might cry or something.

"You O.K.?"

"Sure," she said. "Are *you?*" she added, her jaded side resurfacing.

"Sure," he lied. Actually, he was worried sick about Cal and this campaign, this tenuous lead they had in the polls, this damn baby gorilla taking over the news, and his inability to get on out the door and begin tacking up signs and posters because she was here wearing these wicker-chair blue sandals and confusing the hell out of him with her vacillating personality.

A heavy gust of wind blew the propped door shut.

"I like October," she said and smiled.

"Why?"

"I don't know."

Nat looked out the window.

"It reminds me of an opening night," she added, "before curtain."

"What does that mean?"

"Anticipation."

"You like anticipation?"

"I'm beginning to think it's the only thing in life. Don't you think it's better to *almost* do something—like kiss somebody. Don't you think that's the real feeling people want? Don't you like to be on the brink?"

"You mean living on the edge?"

"No, I'm not talking about things in general. I mean *moments.* I'm talking about sensations—the way your legs feel like Jell-O when you hear your cue and move toward stage or close your eyes and feel somebody's face coming into yours. You know?"

Nat shook his head and avoided her eyes. He wasn't about to let her see his vulnerability.

Whitney drove Francy home. They had delivered yard signs to the people who had responded yes to the following phone-bank questions: Have you given thought to the upcoming congressional vote? Have you made a decision as to who you will support? Would you mind telling me whether or not Calvin Gaines is your choice? Would you be willing to have us place a sign in your front yard?

At Francy's apartment, Whitney told her goodbye and headed home. She was feeling bad because of something she'd said to Nat, and that was the thing about closing your eyes right before you get kissed. She never closed her eyes. An open eye, she felt, was a good thing. "The only safe way to travel," she said aloud. Then she turned on the radio. It was a local phone-in-your-comments show. The topic was embryo ethics. She turned it off.

When she turned into their driveway, she saw Cal and Mary Ellen in the front yard raking leaves. It was something—the way they looked in their white wind-breakers, and she imagined what it was going to be like for them to leave here and move to Washington.

She waved.

Cal put his rake down and approached her. "There's a letter here," he said, opening the screened-porch door. "From yesterday's mail we never brought in."

Whitney took it.

New York postmark, Sam's address but not his writing.

She opened it.

First, she read it silently, then she handed it to Cal, who was standing there trying to look preoccupied with the way the paint was peeling on the banister.

"You want me to read it?" he asked.

She gave him a look. "No, I want you to make a paper airplane with it."

He patted the top of her head affectionately, then read Aaron's letter.

They sat in the rockers for a while. It was dusk. Mary Ellen was raking rhythmically, her head tilted slightly in a pose that told Whitney her mother was discussing a bittersweet topic with God.

"Mom's communing," she said to Cal.

He smiled. "She's got a direct line."

"That carpenter who joined the church last month, you know who I mean?" she asked Cal.

"Yes."

"He said in Sunday School that he prays with his social security number. He says, 'Hi. It's me, 422-87-9043. He says it helps him feel relaxed—like he's got this personal joke with God."

Cal nodded like it made perfect sense.

"I think that's weird," she said.

Cal, still holding Aaron's letter, gestured to it. "What are you going to do about this?"

"Write to her, I guess." What choice was there? It was not in the least an unfamiliar role for her to play—comforting the bereaved—but this was a new ballgame. This was her grandmother. Her grandmother she'd never met, never even knew she had until this year, the mother of her father who lived with a man named Aaron who'd written her this letter.

"Do you think Aaron is Sam's lover?" she asked Cal.

"I don't know."

"Doesn't it seem like he probably is? They've been living together for ten years."

"It would stand to reason."

"If I write to her, then I'm stepping into, as Mom would say, *a relationship.*"

"All to gain, nothing to lose," Cal said.

Whitney stared ahead to the yard, Mary Ellen, the sidewalks and street—all tinted with the mauve color of approaching darkness. She wasn't sure that she agreed with Cal. He, and Mary Ellen, too, lived what he'd just said as a kind of creed. They looked at people as potential relationships. They walked through life like sleepwalkers, their arms forever extended before them, reaching to touch whatever came into the path of their journey. Whitney knew, guiltily, that she was not like them. To get involved is to step into unfamiliar territory, she believed. She did consider herself an explorer. An adventure was an overwhelmingly good thing, but only if it was a solitary pursuit. It wasn't that she feared terrain, only people. Ties developed during a play or an orienteering trip were O.K. because they were, by their nature, temporary.

"You wouldn't have believed the number of workers at the meeting," she told Cal.

"Good. That's encouraging."

"Are you going to win? Do you think you're going to win?"

"Yes," he said.

Whitney went inside. Supper was on the stove where it always was. Mary Ellen always prepared the last meal of the day early so that Cal and Whitney and she could eat whenever they chose. If the mood hit them simultaneously, fine—they ate as a family. If not, nobody felt forced to make a big deal, a ritual, out of dinner. They had enough ceremonies to attend to. Whitney took the lid off the pot. Homemade vegetable soup and French bread. A note on the stove read, "Cal and Whitney, Salad in refrig. M.E." Whitney saw that it was her favorite—congealed with pineapple bits and pecans. She ate three helpings and a lot of bread. She didn't eat any vegetable soup. Once, Mary Ellen had gone on a vegetarian kick. It lasted almost a month. It was awful. Whitney and Cal started eating sausage and biscuits at McDonald's on the way to school and work, and every evening Cal sneaked in a sack of Dino's hotdogs that he and Whitney surreptitiously devoured on the front porch after eating token servings of beans and rice or tofu salad.

Whitney stepped down into the sunken den, sat at Cal's desk, and turned on the lamp. A blank sheet of paper and pen were there beside his old manual typewriter. Cal always left it this way so that, she assumed, he'd have everything ready when an idea hit him for a sermon or book or letter. She felt somewhat displaced; she always wrote in her own bedroom, but she knew she was going to write in here this time. Over her, on the wall, was a print done by a Salvadoran artist named Fernando Llort. It was a woman's profile with various objects ascended over her head—a house, a ball, a plant, a butterfly. It was titled "La Ventana." Whitney told Eva she was real sorry that Hazel had died. She acknowledged that she certainly didn't know Hazel or, for that matter, Eva either, but that she was still sorry. She further acknowledged that she hadn't yet lost anybody to death and didn't know what it felt like, but still she was sorry Eva did have to know. Then she told Eva about her other grandmothers—that Mary Ellen's mother had died before she, Whitney, was born, and Cal's mother had died when she was seven. So Eva was her only living grandmother. She talked about Sam and Aaron, how they were coming, she hoped, to Birmingham the week after the election. Then she said she wanted to meet Eva. She said it was getting to be fairly evident that Diana wasn't going to get in touch, but that was O.K. because she had Eva instead and she was real happy thinking about talking to her. Did she have a family tree? Who was Eva's mother? What was her name and what color were her eyes?

SEVENTEEN

Eva stood at the sink, letting the water run over the mess of turnip greens she'd picked that morning. From the kitchen window, she watched the movers as they hauled Hazel's furniture, piece by piece, from her house and into the van. Eva felt it rising in her—a bit of joy— and turned again to Whitney's letter that she'd placed on the chopping board. She was carrying it virtually everywhere she went. The sight of the movers did not faze her. She smiled, even, thinking about Hazel's things being toted into the new nursing home near Camden, the sweet, curious faces of the old residents who would see it all coming in.

Earlier that week, the redhead from the Curl Up and Dye had knocked on Eva's door, introduced herself, and accepted Eva's invitation to come in for tea. Her name was Becky. Eva found her to be an exceptionally bright and industrious person, a Vietnam War–widow. She was commuting to the junior college, where she was taking various courses, "trying to find something interesting to do in life," she said. She wanted to transfer to the University next year. She had a son, almost grown. As it turned out, Hazel had sort of adopted her and had given her more than a list of customers. Three days before Hazel died, she'd called her attorney, Judson Carmichael, and had him come to the hospital where Hazel instructed him that her house was to go to Becky, though the furniture was to go to the nursing home. "She'd assumed I'd want to sell the house and take the money, according to the attorney," Becky told Eva. But she and her son had decided to move in for a while, at least for a year. She planned to move their things in first of November. As she and Eva parted, Becky took Eva's hand. "Neighbor," she said and smiled. It was a solid handshake, the kind Eva liked in a woman.

And now, today, this letter from Whitney. Eva put the turnip greens in her iron pot and lit the gas burner. She got a pen and the lavender stationery given to her by the Sunday School class on her last birthday. "Old lady stationery," she said aloud, running her fingers over the raised scalloped edges. "Grandmother stationery," she said. She tried to begin the letter, but she wasn't sure what to say.

She went to the phone and dialed New York. Sam's recorded voice came on. "Neither Sam Kirby nor Aaron Wallis is available. If you'd like to leave your name and number, we will return your call."

Eva cleared her throat. "Hi. It's Mom. I don't know which one of you told her, but I got a letter from her today. She's expecting you—*both* of you—in November. Only three weeks away. Call when you have your flight number." Then she dialed the library in Selma. "Archives, please." When the clerk answered, Eva told him she wanted to know how to begin tracing her ancestry. "It's something I'm doing for my granddaughter," she said, knowing the clerk could have cared less.

"What is she saying?" Sam asked Aaron. Eva's message came on right after one from Sam's agent. Sam played it over. "I got the last part—she's saying she has a letter from Whitney and that she's expecting us in November. What's this, though? Listen."

Aaron took off his coat and hung it in the closet. He hadn't told Sam that he'd written Whitney.

"She's saying she doesn't know which one of us wrote to Whitney to tell her Hazel had died. Obviously, it was me."

"*You* wrote *Whitney?*"

Aaron knew that the look Sam wore now meant one of two things. Either he was going to make an angry speech or he was going to hug Aaron fiercely. Sam's volatile nature was exhausting but intriguing, and Aaron knew he was addicted to it. "Not one of the healthier things about me," he'd told Nan, his best friend.

Sam still had on his coat. He was sitting in a chair, bending forward, elbows on thighs—a big bear ready to lunge. Aaron leaned back against the closed closet door.

"Well?" Aaron said.

Sam looked at him. "What made you do that?"

"It was one night after Eva called. It was the night after she'd been to Hazel's graveside service. You weren't here. I was trying to do something to make Eva feel better."

Sam held Aaron with his eyes.

"Stop glaring at me," he said.

"I'm not glaring. I'm gazing," Sam said.

"I don't know what you're thinking," Aaron told him.

"And so now I'm supposed to tell you that I'm think-ing?'"

Aaron shrugged. "Whatever you want."

"Oh, come sit down."

Aaron went to the other chair and rested his hands on the table. "I wish you'd take off your coat," he said.

Sam took it off and tossed it to the sofa. He was wearing a heavy brown sweater—the same color as his eyes. Aaron liked this sweater. It was the first time Sam had worn it this season.

"Are you hungry?" Sam asked him.

"No."

Sam got up and went to the refrigerator. Aaron had gone to the store today. He knew Sam liked the looks of a full refrigerator. "Damn, I don't know where to start," Sam said, into the refrigerator. He opened the cabinet and returned to the table with a can of cashews.

"Well?" Aaron said.

"Well what?"

"Is everything O.K.?"

Sam munched on the cashews and didn't say any-thing. Finally, he looked squarely at Aaron. "That was a nice thing for you to do," he said. "You're really a bet-ter son than me."

Aaron eyed him. He wasn't sure if this was said genu-inely or with facetiousness.

Sam got up, went to his desk, and returned with a calendar and Whitney's last letter.

"Three weeks from Sunday," he said. "She wants us to drive up on Sunday morning and meet her in front of her father's church. 'By the fountain,' as she puts it. I guess that means we'll fly in to Mom's on Saturday, spend the night, and drive to Birmingham early Sun-day. So," Sam said a put a hand on Aaron's, "why don't you write to her and tell her we'll be there."

Aaron looked at him. Sam was smiling warmly. Aaron guessed everything was all right now, or at least Sam was acting like it was since he had something he wanted Aaron to do for him.

"Sure, I'll write to her. She might think it kind of odd, though—me responding to her letter to you."

"It's not any more odd than you writing to tell her Hazel died." Sam shook his head. "I can't get over you doing that."

"What's so strange about it?"

"Well, she probably got a strong hint about us."

"So? I can hardly imagine you hiding that from her."

Sam reddened. "I don't care what she knows. I'm not sure I like Cal knowing."

"So what if he knows?"

Sam's face showed his discomfort, but Aaron wasn't going to drop the subject. He was tired of evading this inevitable conversation. "Well? So what if he knows, too?" he repeated.

Sam's jaw was working.

"Why should you care?" Aaron persisted. "He's *her* father, not *yours.*"

He'd been wanting to say that for months.

"If I want a therapist, I'll go pay for one."

"If anybody in the world ever needed one, it's you," Aaron said quietly.

Sam got his coat and headed for the door. "I'm going for a walk," he said.

Aaron went to the kitchen and made some hot tea. Then he went to the bedroom, sat on the bed, and called his friend, Nan. "I think Sam's coming unraveled," he told her. And, to answer her subsequent question, he responded, "No. It's *good.*"

Aaron wrote to Whitney a day later. Sam knew, though, when he received a letter from her the follow-

ing Friday, that Aaron's letter hadn't reached her prior
to the writing of this, her letter, to Sam. She made no
mention of it and, from her remarks, their plans for
meeting in Birmingham in November were still tentative. She devoted the first paragraph to these loose
ends, her desire for Sam and Aaron to come, and her
anticipation of hearing from him.

The second part of her letter was all about Cal.
There was another article, but Sam saw immediately
that this one was hard news rather than a local descrip-
tion of Cal's ministry. According to the clip, the Central
American refugees for whom Cal's church had been
providing sanctuary had all been deported.

Sam looked at his nails. They needed clipping. He
ran his fingers over the angled drafting table and readjusted the gooseneck lamp. He switched on the lightboard and looked at yesterday's work, illuminated. He
reread the deportation news, then he turned on the
lightboard and looked at what he'd done, illuminated,
on the religious left. He picked up the pieces, one by
one, some of them still on vellum paper and some
transposed onto Bristol board. He turned his chair
around to the big army-green filing cabinet, opened
the double-doors, and put the work into a section at the
bottom of the cabinet reserved for Things I Thought
Were Good While I Was Doing Them, But Actually
Don't Want To See For A Few Years. At the bottom of
the stack was the scrapbook of sorts that Eva had com-
piled at the time Sam considered to be his mother's low
point in life—right after his father died. The book was
a kind of biography, beginning with a photograph of
Sam, Sr., as an infant. He wore a bonnet and looked
feminine, which Sam found interesting and amusing.
Under the photo, Eva had written "Samuel Dean Kirby,
Born 1919." There were some grade-school pictures,
then, with dates underneath. In each one, Sam believed
his father looked increasingly shy and baffled until the
one dated 1943, which showed his father in uniform,

triumphant. Here Eva had written a sentimental, war-years narrative. And then came the Southern Theological Seminary in Kentucky, and Sam was certain there was a marked change in his father's eyes—a reclusive, mean darkness to his face, which was identical to the visual image Sam carried in his own mind when recalling his father. When Aaron came home that evening after work, Sam showed him the scrapbook and asked if he recognized the change.

Aaron was carrying a sack of groceries and wore a look of mild bewilderment. It was then that Sam remembered their having had words with one another last night and that they hadn't spoken since. Sam had been asleep when Aaron left for work.

Sam took the groceries from Aaron and removed his camel-colored tam. This was intended as a gentle act of reconciliation—a small gesture to match what Sam considered the small nature of their spat last night. Sam looked down into the sack—celery, pasta, apples, and juice.

"Come over here," Sam urged, setting the sack on the table.

Aaron kept eyeing him warily.

"What is it?" Sam asked. "Are you mad?"

"No. Are you?"

"Look," Sam said. "Don't you think his face changes in this picture?"

Sam held a chair out, motioning for Aaron to join him at the table. He kept his finger on the photograph of his father. Aaron sighed and tilted his head to one side as if considering.

"He looks more serious," he said finally.

Sam looked at it again. "But don't you think he looks mean? Don't you think he looks like a nice guy, up to this point?"

Aaron got up and began opening cabinets, putting the groceries away.

"Did you have a good day?" Aaron asked him.

"Yeah. You?"

"Nan and I were talking today," Aaron said.

Sam waited. He knew this meant they had been dissecting—their—Sam and Aaron's—relationship between therapy sessions with clients. Sam raised an eyebrow, to say, "And?"

"We were thinking it's sad that Diana won't be there with you in Birmingham to meet Whitney."

Sam nodded, prepared to hear the rest of the bullshit.

"You know, that would be something for you to all be together."

"A family," Sam said flatly.

"Right," Aaron said with sincerity.

"Reunited," Sam added.

Aaron looked at him. "Are you really agreeing with me?"

"Sure," Sam said. He hated to make light of Aaron's thoughts or to belittle his profession and his friendship with Nan, but this ranked with the more ludicrous of Aaron's and Nan's analyses. *Re*united. As if they'd been united, as if Whitney's conception was any more than the byproduct of a sadly hilarious final night with a woman. The details of it were beginning to come into the realm of recall.

E IGHTEEN

Whitney woke early. The light in her bedroom was somewhere between gray and pink.
It was raining. Nat had told her, "Pray for sunshine. Rain always means bad news for our
party." Whitney hadn't pursued this and now
wished she had, because along with her panic
over the weather was a feeling of confusion
over what it all meant—this precipitation factor. She showered and put on a lot of make-up
and cologne. She knew this was quite contrary
to her new idea of herself as earth-person, but
it made her feel more worldly and less trans-

parent. By the time she descended the stairs, she already heard Cal, Mary Ellen, Francy, and Nat in the kitchen, laughing, dishes clattering, bacon frying—like they'd all awoke jubilant and half-crazed from a wild slumber party. Nat's dark hair was wet and kinky. Francy had on a raincoat. It was election day.

"Morning sweetie," Mary Ellen said. She wore an apron that one of the Hispanic women had given her. It was a print of a giant tropical bird. Mary Ellen turned the bacon.

"Did y'all spend the night here?" Whitney asked Francy and Nat, gesturing to the clock on the wall. It was six-thirty a.m.

Francy gave Whitney a little bear hug. "No. We've been up most of the night, though."

The way she said "we" caused Whitney to believe, for an awful instant, that Nat might have spent the night at Francy's. Whitney glanced over to where Nat stood, wet, in his old tight jeans—the ones Whitney had grown to anticipate and like.

Cal was standing over a wet newspaper that was spread open on the kitchen table. He was wearing a red, green, and blue plaid shirt and faded khakis. He looked like a fashionable outdoorsman—a kind of look she'd seen in some magazine. Cal's face was bright with merriment, and Nat, too, was obviously in on the mirth she didn't understand. Mary Ellen, apparently sensing her confusion, said, "We're laughing at the front page of the paper, sweetie."

Whitney went over, stood by Cal, and looked. The headline read, "Name-the-Gorilla-Contest Winner Named." There was a big photograph of the baby gorilla with a caption that said "Enoch." Beside Enoch's picture was one of a girl who looked younger than Whitney. The caption read, "Susan Austin, Winner." The headlines, pictures, and story took up most of the front page.

"Great campaign coverage," Nat said to Whitney.

She smiled. She looked again at the baby gorilla. He really was cute.

"I can't believe it," Francy said. "Not even a little front-page blurb."

"It is an off-year," Mary Ellen noted. "No presidential race to make election day seem like a *real* election day.

Francy set the table. She knew exactly where to locate the silverware, salt and pepper shakers, butter dish, and juice glasses. She and Mary Ellen worked in rhythm, dodging one another in a kind of domestic dance—one that Whitney had observed in church women over the years as they traveled in and out of each other's kitchens, preparing food and serving it to their children, neighbors, strangers, and aliens. The dance had an element of grace most all the time, with the possible exception of soup-line duty. In the hot basement kitchen of Cal's church, Mary Ellen, Francy, and the others were prone to wear bandanas, bland aprons, and glistening foreheads as they danced in a more exact tempo, conscious of each measured serving. Here, this morning, though, it was the old family waltz, and Whitney joined alongside Francy and her mother, reaching in the cabinets for plates, buttering the toast, pouring the juice.

Cal read from the Bible—the psalm about, "When I consider the heavens, the moon and the stars, what is man?"—and then said his usual morning prayer of gratitude as if today were just another normal day, when in actuality Whitney knew their lives might be changed forever by seven o'clock this evening. She shivered involuntarily at the thought just as Cal ended his prayer. Mary Ellen looked at her, having seen the shiver. They both chuckled, and Cal, Nat, and Francy looked up questioningly. Mary Ellen waved it away. "Whitney and I are just on the same wavelength, that's all," she explained.

"Which one is that?" Cal asked, and passed the huge

platter that held the bacon, scrambled eggs, and toast.

"The election-day jitters," Mary Ellen said.

Cal put one hand on Mary Ellen's, the other on Whitney's. "All things work together for the good of those who love God," he said.

Whitney gave him an "Oh-please-spare-us" kind of look.

"I'm sorry," he told her.

She patted his hand tenderly. "It's O.K. I know you only talk that way when you're nervous."

Francy giggled and nodded her agreement to Whitney's statement.

"Or when he's depressed," Mary Ellen noted.

"Or when he's gotten busy with something secular and suddenly feels that he needs to pay homage to his profession. I've noticed that, too," Francy said.

Cal put his fork down. "Listen. You're all like some interdisciplinary treatment team, discussing my case. *He* does this, *he* does that. Isn't that what they're doing?" he asked Nat. "Don't you think I'm doing great? Don't you think I've maintained a well-balanced state of mental health through extraordinary circumstances?"

Nat raised a wary eyebrow.

"Well?" Cal pressed Nat. "What was that? What's that look supposed to mean?"

Nat leaned forward, over his plate. "You are a wreck, Cal."

Francy giggled again. Whitney noted that nobody had eaten a bite, except for her. She was very hungry.

"But it's O.K.," Nat continued. "It's normal. No serious candidate wakes on election morning with a song in his heart."

"I like that," Whitney said.

Nat was beside her. He turned and caught her gaze for a moment. His eyes, then, did something funny. They were like ice cubes melting in the sun. It was then she understood that she and Nat were dancing. She

liked the dance. It resembled the domestic dance of
southern women because it was unconscious and unob-
ligatory—just some morning you're in somebody else's
kitchen, handling their dishes with familiarity and easi-
ness, glancing at their clock, and opening their cabinets. It lacked the concreteness, though, of this mutual
chosen servitude. It was abstract, Whitney felt. It had
no design. It was unacknowledged. The dance existed
only in invisible symbols and movement. Because of its
intangible nature, it might be love. Love, Whitney felt,
was a very heavy word, though. It wasn't part of her
everyday vocabulary, either aloud or silently. She didn't
like to use it unless the situation demanded it, and the
situation usually didn't.

The polls had Cal in the lead. It was marginal, but
still it was a lead, enough to make you believe you're
actually going to win. "Nat has a great sense of pace,"
Francy told Whitney. "He's like an experienced runner.
He'll let it all loose at the end." Nat had saved practically a stockroom-full of signs, and on election eve, his
Union buddies had staked them every hundred yards
or so in the grassy medians of the three major Interstate arteries that fed into the city's business district.

After breakfast, Francy had said, "Come on, I want
to take you for a drive."

And now, they were riding along I-65, and "Calvin
Gaines for Congress" was engraving itself into her
head. Whitney rolled down her window and let the
chilly November air hit her face. She felt real good. She
looked over at Francy who was chewing gum feverishly.
Francy's prescription sunglasses had an FK monogram
at the temple. Whitney was certain Francy was gaining
weight, but she didn't want to say anything.

"We're going to win, aren't we?" Whitney said.

"Sure," Francy answered cheerfully.

Just then, Whitney was seized with a startling question.

"Francy! What'll happen to you? What will you do?"

"I'm moving to Washington, hon." Francy turned and smiled radiantly, her seagull earrings flying in the wind.

Whitney settled herself back into her seat. Of course. She realized that Cal must have talked with Francy about this long ago, probably when he first decided to run.

"Francy Krueger. Congressional secretary," Whitney said.

"Sounds a lot better than church secretary, doesn't it?" Francy asked.

"Yeah, it does."

Francy exited the Interstate and let Whitney off at the University's Humanities Building, where her morning classes were being held. She'd parked her bicycle in the rack before her ride with Francy, and she noted that it was still there, chained up. Most of her friends had gone off to "good schools" to study art or drama or music, but she was happy going here for now. She liked the idea of an urban university where nobody took themselves seriously. And anyway, everything might change after today.

After her early-evening Earth Science lab, she pedaled home to change clothes before going to headquarters for the returns. The neighborhood was soothing in its familiarity. She knew these streets and avenues like the back of her hand. The moon was bright. Venus was, too. Victory. She rode faster. By the time she parked her bicycle in the carport, she was breathless. Mary Ellen had left some spaghetti on the stove. She turned on the TV and began untying her shoelaces. Election results were coming in. There were a lot of seats up this year, all over the country. The major networks were all covering it. She listened while she bathed, put on a pair of Mary Ellen's earrings, and heated up the spaghetti. It was only eight o'clock. "The District 6 race in Alabama," the anchorman began. Whitney put the hotpad down and turned the TV up. "The religious right versus the religious left race that made recent news with the incumbent's challenger refusing to deny his active role in the Sanctuary Movement has apparently been decided. We are projecting Albert Naylor the winner."

Whitney didn't move. Her heart was racing. She flipped the TV off and stepped into the den. She sat on the edge of the sofa. She waited. She was waiting for something to happen. This just wasn't any good at all. She wasn't even at headquarters yet. She was here, alone. She went upstairs. First, she went to her room and looked in the mirror. Her face was awful-looking. It was all drained and sad. Then she went into her parents' bedroom. It was in perfect order. On Mary Ellen's vanity were the usual things that Whitney had loved to play with as a child—an old, real-ivory comb-and-brush set, a handmade plaster-of-paris dish holding rings that Mary Ellen never wore, and a framed photograph of Cal, taken when he was a chaplain in the army—probably the year she was born. She held it. She cried.

Some of the campaign workers were moving dreamily, as though they were sleepwalking or floating. Still, they had smiles. Whitney glanced back at her mother's car, which she'd parked illegally by a fire hydrant. What the hell? She spotted her mother in a corner, wearing a white dress, looking like an incredible angel. "Here's Whitney," she saw her mother's mouth say to whoever was near. And Mary Ellen's face opened into a great smile.

"I've already heard," Whitney said.

Mary Ellen gave her a little hug, one that said, "Don't worry, I'm not going to give you an emotional piece of myself." Whitney knew her mother knew that she had a hard time dealing with big feelings, be they good or bad. She'd scrubbed her face over and over so that nobody would know she'd cried, and she sure as hell wasn't going to cry here. It took all her might, though, when she saw Cal talking into a camera, wearing his look of God-Is-Here-At-This-Moment-Helping-Me-Through-This-Crisis.

Finally, the strong camera lights went away, and he turned and saw Whitney. He approached her, and she shrank back to avoid his arms. Sensing her vulnerability, he just gently took her hand, as he would with someone who was visiting the church. In fact, she could almost hear him say, "Are you looking for a church-home?" This made her laugh, then she had to fight a kind of giddiness that made her tremble.

"Like to get out of here?" Cal asked her.

She nodded.

Cal opened the headquarters door, smiling to a new group of TV people who had just arrived. He waved, then led Whitney by the arm along the sidewalk.

"Mom's car is right here," she said. "I parked illegally."

Cal grinned. "A family of lawbreakers," he said.

She returned the smile and got in the passenger's side.

Cal turned on the ignition. Whitney rolled down her window, and the cool night air filled the car.

"November's a great month," she said.

"You like elections?"

"Is that a serious question?" she asked him.

Cal stopped for a red light at the star intersection, Five Points.

"Are you all right?" he asked her.

"Sure."

He turned to her, his face pained. "You always say sure. I've never quite been able to read you. I never know if you're truly O.K."

"What difference does it make if I'm O.K. or not O.K.? In the end, everything's always the same anyway. I mean, if I'm not O.K. tonight, I'll probably be O.K. in the morning. Nobody stays permanently 'not O.K.'"

"I just love you, that's all," he said.

Whitney turned away and looked out the car window. They passed the hardware store that had donated the nails for the signs. They passed Cal's church. They passed the ice cream shop, bars, a bicycle repair place, the new exercise studio. She knew she was supposed to say, "I love you, too," to Cal. She didn't understand the thing in her that always stopped her from saying it.

"I'm glad you ran," she said.

"You are?" Cal pulled over and parked in an empty parking lot behind a new hotel. They were near downtown, now. He grabbed the sleeve of her windbreaker. "You really are glad? You mean that?"

"Sure."

"Why are you glad?"

She didn't know how to answer that. A couple passed by, having emerged from the entrance on the side of the hotel. The man was wearing a business suit, and his red tie was askew. The woman had on a glittery dress and was waving a cigarette. "I hope she doesn't burn him with that," Whitney said, gesturing to the woman.

"Why are you glad?" Cal persisted.

"I had fun."

"You had fun," Cal repeated.

"Yes."

"What else?"

"I met a lot of interesting people."

"Who? Who was interesting?"

Whitney shrugged. "Yarbrough's daughter from the zoo. She has tattoos."

Cal gave her a You're Kidding look.

"Yes," Whitney said. "She has chrysanthemum tattoos growing up from here," she said, spreading her hands over her breasts. "She has a rose on her ankle. She got the tattoos in Germany."

Cal tapped the steering wheel with his fingers.

"How old were you in that picture Mom has on her vanity?"

Cal looked up, calculating. "Twenty-three, maybe."

"I was looking at it before I left home," she said.

Cal smiled and said nothing.

Whitney looked at her hands.

"I heard the projection on TV while I was heating the spaghetti."

Cal stared ahead. The couple had stopped by a car. The man was forcing the woman up against it, pressing his body into hers.

"I never did get to eat," Whitney continued.

Cal halfway smiled. Whitney couldn't tell if he was looking at the couple or just considering what she was saying.

"It startled me," she said. "It surprised me that they'd have a projection so early. Are those projections right?"

"Usually," Cal said.

"What happened?"

"You mean why did we lose?"

"Yes," she said, "when the polls had you ahead. Was it the rain this morning?"

Cal shrugged. "I doubt if the rain lost the election."

"Well, what then?"

"I don't know," Cal said. "It was always very close, you know. It's hard to beat an incumbent."

"But he's only been there for one term."

"The district is changing. It doesn't know who it wants to be."

Whitney didn't understand this totally.

"Things may turn over a few times during the next several years. We do have a black mayor."

"So?"

"So, that's progress, don't you think?"

"I went upstairs after I heard the projection," Whitney said. "I went to my room, then I went to yours and Mom's room. That's when I saw the picture."

Cal looked at her.

"I was thinking maybe it was taken the year you got me."

"I can't recall," Cal said.

"That was something," Whitney said. "You getting me."

Cal smiled. "Yeah, that was something."

"I mean, it was something that you would do that for me."

Cal looked at her searchingly. "Well, we wanted you."

She put a knuckle to her lips. Cal started the car. She knew he was doing this for her, she knew he knew she was getting uncomfortable, getting into the danger zone—the one that had Diana in the question mark nucleus.

"Well, do you feel *rejected?*" she asked forcefully.

"Because I lost?"

"Yeah."

"Sure," he replied.

"I hate that feeling," she said.

"Me, too," he said.

"I hate it with a passion," she declared and hung her arm out the window.

NINETEEN

By Friday, Nat had most of the campaign paraphernalia gathered up and disposed of. On the way over to the Gaineses', he stopped at the donut shop, got a morning paper, and went inside. He sat at the counter and ordered three raspberry donuts and a cup of black coffee. He looked at the front page of the newspaper. The headline read, "Zoological Society Members Outraged." Enoch, the baby gorilla, was being temporarily separated from his mother, who was being transported to the New Orleans Zoo for a new mating. Nat smiled. He was taking Whitney to the zoo this morning to see Enoch. He'd taken the day off from work.

Whitney was on the front porch when he arrived. She was in jeans and wore a turquoise sweater that made her eyes look like Caribbean waters. She was in the rocker, legs up on the banister.

"Hi," she said and got up from her rocker. "I'm ready. Mom and Dad aren't here. You didn't need to see them, did you?"

"No. No more business to tend to."

She looked at him. "The campaign being over doesn't mean anything, does it? You'll still be around."

"Sure."

"Well, I hope so. Dad needs you."

Nat opened the car door, and she slid in. He walked to the other side and zipped up his jacket. Winter was coming, making its usual snail-paced movement into Alabama.

"What did you mean by that?" he asked.

"By Dad needing you?"

"Yeah."

"He doesn't have a man friend that I know of. There are plenty of church friends, sure, but they don't count."

"No?"

"They're parishioners. He can't be himself, you know."

"Well, I'm sure not going anywhere," Nat said. "I'll be around. I like Cal. I like Cal a lot."

"Have you talked to Francy?" Whitney asked.

"Yeah. We talked last night."

"Where did you talk?" Whitney asked.

"At my place," he said.

"At your place?"

Nat looked at her. He thought for a hopeful moment that she sounded jealous. "She stopped by with five hundred nails. She wondered if we should return them to the hardware store or give them to some carpenter who joined your church last month."

"He's the guy who prays with his social security number," Whitney said.

"What?"

Whitney waved it away. "Forget it," she said. "It's just a weird church thing."

"I'm thinking about joining," Nat said. He had imagined himself sharing a hymnal with Whitney. It was, without a doubt, the most adolescent kind of daydream he'd had since he passed sixteen.

"You'll have to get dunked," Whitney warned. She laughed. "I can't picture you in the baptismal water, Dad holding your nose with a handkerchief."

"What?"

"That's what he does before he puts somebody under."

Nat hadn't considered this aspect of it.

"Do you have to be saved to join?" he asked her.

She held her palms up. "Don't ask me."

"Are you saved?"

She grinned, then turned to the window. A while later, she turned back to him. "Some people think being saved means you're living in a state of grace. Do you know what grace means?"

"No."

"It means you get an unasked for, undeserved gift."

Nat nodded.

"If that's what being saved is," she continued, "the answer to your questions is yes. I was saved the day Mom and Dad got me."

Nat drove by the zoo entrance and parked beside a picnic table and some trees. They got out of the car and walked toward the gate.

"That was fun the day we came out here to Yarbrough's place," she said.

"Was it?"

"Yeah. Didn't you think so?" She turned to him. He started to tell her that her eyes were like sunlit Caribbean waters, but he knew that would be a mistake. She hated poetry, and she probably hated similes. They passed the flamingos, peacocks, and ostriches. The sea lions were being fed. He and Whitney were the only people around. "Breakfast," the zoo worker called to the animals. After they ate, the sea lions resumed their languid, circular swim around the concrete island in the middle of their pool.

"Incredible," Whitney said. She shook her head. "You know they're smarter than we are."

Nat didn't know anything about animals, and except for the trip to Yarbrough's he hadn't been to the zoo in twenty years.

"Where's Enoch?" Whitney called to the zoo person who was still standing on the sea lions' concrete island.

He pointed east. "Over in that pavilion," he called.

Enoch was behind a glass wall, wearing a disposable diaper just like he'd worn in the newspaper photograph. A male nurse, wearing surgical scrub clothes, was attending him. Actually, the guy was reading a newspaper and drinking something from a thermos at a tiny desk inside the glass cage.

"Round-the-clock nurses," Whitney said, "from Children's Hospital."

"Yeah, that's what I hear," Nat said.

Whitney put her palms against the glass. Enoch rolled a beach ball over to where she stood and put his hands on the glass, against hers. She put her nose on the pane, then her lips. Nat turned away and walked in the direction of the elephants.

"I lost you," she said and smiled. She pushed her turquoise sweater sleeves up her thin arms. The day was warming up a bit.

"Well, what did you think of him?" Nat asked her.

"He's great. I think he wants out of his glass cage, though."

"You want to see anything else?" he asked, looking up at the elephants. They were standing perfectly still.

"You need to be somewhere?'" she asked. "Are you in a hurry?"

"No."

"You always seem like you're in a hurry."

They sat on top of a concrete picnic table and rested their feet on the bench below.

Nat looked up. "Maples," he said, "and that's a mulberry tree over there."

"How can you tell?"

"The shape of the leaves and also the trunk. See how it bends forward? It has a curve. Grace. Some trees, like those white oaks over there, see, look like men to me. I always thought mulberry trees were kind of feminine."

Whitney looked at him vacantly. Nat assumed she was bored.

"Do you think we're dancing?" she asked him.

He felt his stomach tighten, but he kept his face straight. "Sure," he said and picked up a piece of pine straw.

"How long do you think we've been dancing?" she asked him.

He looked at the pine straw, then pulled it apart.

"A year?" he said.

"You mean since the campaign started?"

"I don't know," he said. "What do you think?"

"I didn't think about it until breakfast the other day. Does that mean that's when it started? Do you think it's not real until you get aware of it?"

Nat looked at his boots. "Well, maybe it goes on a long time before you realize it. Then, in retrospect..."

"But when did you know it?" she asked.

"What is *it,* anyway?'" he asked, still looking down at his boots, the concrete bench, the pine straw.

"The dance."

"Oh."

"Well?"

"The night at the steel-plant party," he said. "You pulled your hair up. It was hot."

"I don't think I was dancing then," she said.

"Well, I was."

"The bad thing about the dance, I think, is that it ends when you acknowledge it," she said.

"Then it's all over?"

"That part is."

"Then what?" he asked.

"I don't know. I've never acknowledged it," she said. "I usually just keep dancing and don't move on to whatever's next."

He wondered if this was some weird way of telling him she was a virgin.

"Are you acknowledging it now?" he asked her.

"Yes."

"Why?" He turned to face her.

"I'm going to the symphony tonight with Mom and Dad."

Nat looked at her.

"Beethoven's Ninth," she said.

He looked unabashedly at her lips.

"I like the ending to it, don't you?"

Nat put his finger on the tip of her nose, then her lips.

"The Joy melody," she said.

He kissed her. The chemistry was right. It felt natural and good, fresh and bold.

The musicians were warming up. Whitney liked the discordant ramblings of the violinists, the way the harpist kept adjusting her body to accommodate her big gold instrument. The principal flutist looked Whitney's age. She had blond hair that cascaded over her prim black dress. They were like actors getting into character. They were, at this moment, still individuals. The conductor wasn't yet on stage to make them into an orchestra. He was new. This was his first year. At the designated moment, the musicians stopped their ramblings, the audience was hushed, and he burst from behind a curtain on the left. He was dark-skinned, strikingly young, and vibrant. Instantly, his arms went up to his orchestra, and they began the opening movement of Beethoven's Ninth Symphony. It was one of the few symphonies with which Whitney was totally familiar. It was like the theme of this first movement was background music for her life—she'd heard it so many times in the sunken den. Cal played it a lot. Whitney glanced over at Cal and Mary Ellen. Their profiles in the semidarkness were all right. They looked intent on the music and perfectly happy, not a trace of worry or fatigue. They were all, now, five days past the election.

During the second movement, she kept her eyes on the conductor. He reminded her of Nat. He was all energy. Whitney thought this was probably his favorite part of the symphony. He looked like a fast-paced man. But, then, during the adagio movement, he melted down and moved his arms in a certain way like all he'd been doing was waiting for this sublime place. It was then that Whitney's mind started wandering just as it did when Cal was halfway through a sermon. She thought of wallpapering her bedroom—now that they weren't moving to Washington. She thought of Nat at the zoo and wondered what on earth was happening with her and him. The campaign was over, but things were still crazy. Sam was coming in the morning, and she was meeting him right outside Cal's church. He was bringing Aaron. They were going to hear Cal preach, then drive down to south Alabama where she was going to meet Eva. She wanted to meet Eva. She wanted to meet Sam, but she was scared. She thought of spring—how the high school had asked her to come back and direct a play of her choice next April. She thought of

TWENTY

Sam parked behind the church. Aaron kept reaching over to pat his shoulder, reassuringly. Sam felt nervous. He couldn't ever remember feeling so nervous. He was wearing a dark-blue suit which certainly didn't help his uneasiness. He and Aaron had left Eva's this morning at seven-thirty. It was almost eleven now. He looked in the rearview mirror one last time.

"You look great," Aaron said. "You look very fatherly."

"This wasn't a good idea," Sam said. "I should have suggested something else. This isn't the place to meet."

They got out of the car.

"Think how she must feel," Aaron said. "It's probably the safest place in the world for her. Don't you think that's why she wanted to do it here?"

"Anybody who feels safe in front of a church in Birmingham," Sam began, but then they rounded the corner, and there was the big fountain she'd described. She was sitting on the ledge, wearing a pastel-colored lightweight coat. She got up as they approached. She smiled warmly into Sam's eyes. It was eerie and incredibly sweet—the sight of her.

"O.K.," she said to both of them. "Who's who?" But, of course, she knew. The resemblance was striking—just as it had been when he first saw the photograph of her. And now, he knew she felt it, too.

"Hi, Aaron," she said and shook Aaron's hand.

She gave Sam a quick hug, then she led them into the church.

Inside, he and Aaron followed her to a pew, and they slid in. She introduced them to the guy next to her, Nat, and then she introduced them to the woman next to Nat, Francy. "Nat was Dad's campaign manager," she said. "Francy's Dad's secretary." Sam felt Aaron's presence as a lifejacket, certain to carry him through the next hour until they were safely back in Eva's car and moving along the Interstate toward home.

"In a minute, the choir will begin the processional,'" she told him. "They'll be coming from behind you. Just wanted to warn you. Sometimes, in the back here, it's real loud—the singing."

A man and woman, Cal and Mary Ellen, he assumed, appeared from a side door in the front and walked toward the big chairs by the pulpit.

"That's Mom and Dad," Whitney told him. Sam knew Cal from the newspaper photographs. Still, he wasn't prepared for his size. He was tall and riveting. Mary Ellen was also extraordinary—radiant and wearing a big, red hat, all smiles. She turned to the left side of the room and began American Sign Language.

"Deaf congregation," Whitney whispered. "That section over there. She's telling them the page number of the opening hymn."

Sam turned to Aaron. "That's her mother."

Aaron watched, obviously fascinated. Sam knew Aaron was probably already planning just the way he'd describe all this to Nan.

The organist chimed eleven notes, and, then, as Whitney had warned, voices bellowed from behind, and the processional began. Everybody stood up, and Whitney's mother was signing like crazy, her hands busily interpreting the lyrics. After this was over, everybody sat down. Cal read something from the Bible, and Sam looked down, trying discreetly to examine Whitney's hands. They didn't look like his. He couldn't remember Diana's hands. All he remembered about Diana's appearance was her long, straight, light-colored hair—the same color as Whitney's. Whitney had Diana's coloring, but the structure of her face was unmistakably Sam's. He glanced at her feet. It was hard to say whose ankles she had. For her sake, he hoped she'd gotten his great legs. Whose mind did she have? Or was that even in question? Was she just a physical being— an infant, the tabula rasa—when these people got her from Diana at the Home in Ft. McClellan? Did his influence end after the moment of conception?

Cal began his sermon.

"I had a phone call Wednesday morning," he began, "the day after the election. It was from our sister church in New Orleans. Brother John Franklin told me, 'Cal, we're relieved you are not going anywhere. We're also relieved the cameras are turning away from Birmingham, and the INS is back in Washington. We have five families waiting. They've been waiting all summer for your defeat. They'll arrive next week.'" Cal went on to say that the families had children, and all were from El Salvador. He gave some morbid details of their lives. "At the end of the service, we'll have an altar call for Sanctuary, and I know you can respond and open your homes just as you've done in the past."

Cal read the thing in Matthew about being "hungry and you fed me, thirsty and you gave me drink, a stranger and you took me in," and all that. Sam vaguely recalled it from childhood. Then he tuned Cal out. He was struck with the beauty of the stained glass. Morning sun fell through the bright red, yellow, and turquoise panes, causing the people to be lit up various colors.

It was windowpane acid that he and Diana were taking the night Whitney was conceived. The night was sloppy. On top of the hallucinogens, there was a good bit of liquor. There were Diana's theater friends all over the house. Or was it an apartment? Was it early evening or dawn? It was August, and it was hot. People were in and out of the place like a colony of ants. The acid, in fact, had the effect of stirring up the ant bed, causing the small creatures—Sam being one—to randomly and sense-lessly crawl all over one another, frenzied and confused. Diana's body was foreign—friendly but alien. He liked her. She was, he was forced to recall, a good person. It's just that he *knew*, with finality, that his body and mind were meant to love men. The glory of this inescapable fact, realizing itself at last, was enough to carry the act on to its culminating release. It wasn't meant to bear fruit, but it had. Whitney was opening her hymnal now, and it was clear that Cal's sermon was concluding. Sam kept his eyes on Mary Ellen's hands, marveling at whatever they were translating. He didn't understand a word, but he knew it was a good thing she was doing.

Finally, it was over.

"I want you to meet Mom and Dad, O.K.? Just for a minute?"

Sam said O.K.

She turned to Aaron. "And will you meet them, too? O.K.?"

The guy next to her—Nat—said something to Whitney that Sam didn't catch. Whitney smiled at Nat and said, "Be home on Tuesday." Then he saw Whitney make meaningful eye contact with her father's secretary. Frances? Was that her name?

Whitney led Sam and Aaron up to where Mary Ellen stood. She was talking in sign language to some people. She smiled, winked at Sam, and held up a finger, like, "Be with you in just a second."

Whitney held Sam's hand lightly.

Cal turned.

"This is Sam," she told Cal. "This is Aaron."

At first, Cal didn't move. Sam hesitated. Aaron raised a hand for shaking, but Cal abruptly took Sam in his right arm, Aaron in his left, and drew them against him. Sam flinched, but Cal stood firm. Gradually, Sam felt his own body losing its resistance, and he allowed himself to be embraced.

"This is Five Points," she said. "This is my stomping ground. It's a funny kind of neighborhood."

"How so?" Aaron asked, from the backseat.

She turned to him. "Different kinds of people."

"So you live around here?" Sam asked her, glancing up at the light that was changing from red to green.

"About a mile up the mountain there. That's Red Mountain," she said. "I guess you know all this? Did you come to Birmingham much when you were growing up?"

"No, we went to Selma whenever we needed a big city."

She smiled. "Selma," she repeated. "I've never been to Selma."

"Well, you're on your way right now," Sam reminded her.

"Yeah."

"What's the best way to get on I-65?" he asked her.

"Take a left at the next light onto Eighth Avenue."

Whitney turned back to Aaron. "Well, how long have you and Sam been together?" she asked him.

Sam felt his neck redden.

"Ten years," Aaron said casually.

"That's a long time," she noted. "Do you ever fight?"

"Never," Aaron said.

They talked about the election. She seemed, to Sam, to be O.K. about the outcome. Eventually, she began asking some vague, innocuous questions about his life at the time of her birth.

"If we had decided against the adoption, we were going to name you Echo."

"Thank God you didn't," she said.

"Everybody was naming their kids things like that," Aaron said to her.

"Like what else?" she asked him.

"Oh, you know. Brook, Free, Sunshine, Patience."

"Peace," Sam added.

"Moon," Aaron said.

"Unit," Sam rejoined.

Sam and Aaron laughed. Whitney smiled with the courtesy of an outsider who doesn't quite understand the joke but is eager to keep the good spirit alive.

Sam drove on. It was some kind of November day. The sky was painfully blue, and he had the sensation of a growing promise. It wasn't until he had gotten off the Interstate, crossed Yellow Leaf Creek, passed the railroad tracks at Jemison, and headed on to Maplesville—that he began to realize what was happening. The trees were changing, losing their barrenness. Back in Birmingham, all the hardwoods were almost bare from pending winter. Farther along, he understood now, they'd begun to show an earlier time in fall. The cold had not quite reached them, and their leaves were still red and gold. And he knew that eventually they would become green, as he traveled south, backward in seasonal time, toward home.

Deep South Books

The University of Alabama Press

VICKI COVINGTON
Gathering Home

VICKI COVINGTON
The Last Hotel for Women

NANCI KINCAID
Crossing Blood